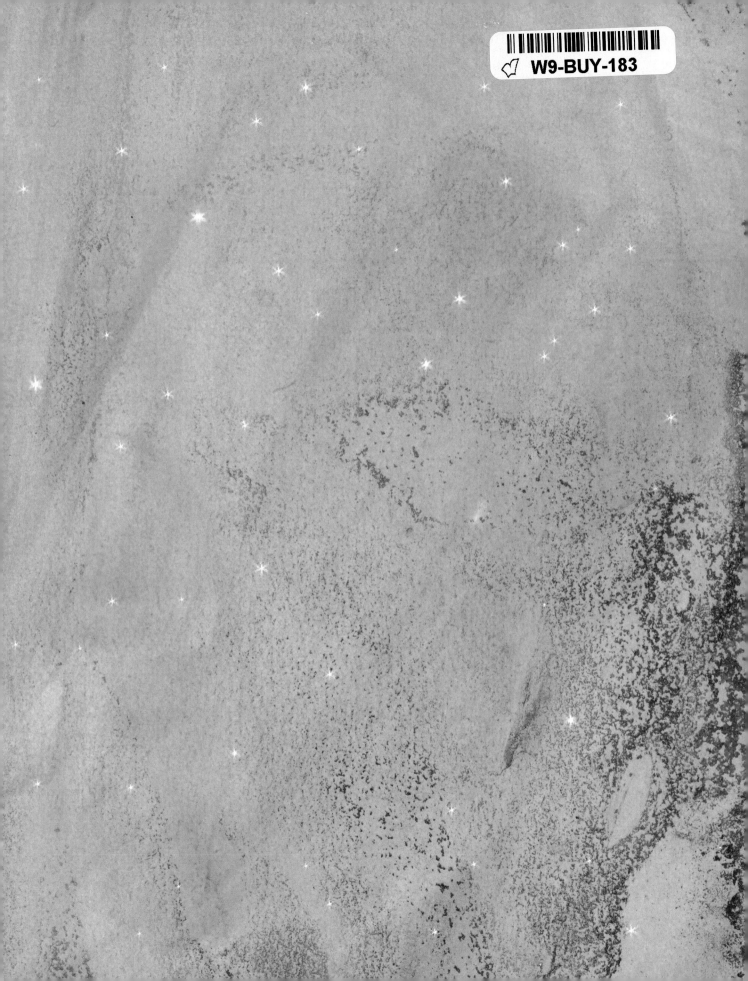

CUENTO
DE LUZ

For Aroa, all of my stories.

A Night Time Story

Text © 2012 Roberto Aliaga
Illustrations © 2012 Sonja Wimmer
This edition © 2012 Cuento de Luz SL
Calle Claveles 10 | Urb Monteclaro | Pozuelo de Alarcón | 28223 Madrid | Spain | www.cuentodeluz.com
Original title in Spanish: Cuento de Noche
English translation by Jon Brokenbrow

ISBN: 978-84-15241-98-0

Printed by Shanghai Chenxi Printing Co., Ltd. in PRC, January 2012, print number 1256-09

FSC
www.fsc.org
MIX
Paper from
responsible sources
FSC® C007923

A Night Time Story

Roberto Aliaga ★ Sonja Wimmer

Every night, before I go to sleep, she sits down on my bed with heaps of stories in her hands. She's got them all.

She tucks my blankets up under my chin.
Then she chooses one at random and, in
a gentle voice, begins to read...

Right away, my bedroom is full of words
and pictures. Because in her stories,
I'm always the main character.

There are **sweet** stories,

like the one when we visit the
fairground in the city. We climb up
onto the Ferris wheel, and she
buys me cotton candy…

There are **_chilly_** stories, like
the one when we go ice skating in
the snow, holding hands…

Some of the stories are *magical*, like the one
when my bed lands in the branches of a tree,
and she teaches me to sing and fly.

Some of them are *scary*.
In one story, a hand comes out from under my bed and pulls off the sheets. It's Matty, my cat, but I don't know that!

There are stories that are *funny*, like the one when we dress up, playing at being someone else, someone we'd like to be.

There are *dark* stories, like the one when I'm looking for her, but I can't find her.

Some of the stories are *mysterious*.
I remember one when my bed rose up like a camel, and we
walked off into the desert in search of a mirage…

And other ones are *perfect*, until I wake up.

Before I go to sleep, the night sits on my bed, with heaps
of dreams in her hands. She's got them all.

She tucks my blankets up under my chin, chooses one at
random and, with her gentle voice, I start to dream…

DOPING
IN SPORTS
WINNING AT ANY COST?

STEPHANIE SAMMARTINO MCPHERSON

TWENTY-FIRST CENTURY BOOKS / MINNEAPOLIS

For all who love sports—
athletes, coaches, and fans alike

Special thanks to my editor, Amy Fitzgerald, for her enthusiasm and invaluable help, and to my husband, Richard, for his suggestions and encouragement

Text copyright © 2016 by Stephanie Sammartino McPherson

Twenty-First Century Books
A division of Lerner Publishing Group, Inc.
241 First Avenue North
Minneapolis, MN 55401 USA

For reading levels and more information, look up this title at www.lernerbooks.com.

Main body text set in Adrianna Regular 10/15.
Typeface provided by Chank.

Library of Congress Cataloging-in-Publication Data

McPherson, Stephanie Sammartino.
    Doping in sports : winning at any cost? / Stephanie Sammartino McPherson.
        pages cm
    Audience: Age 12–18.
    Audience: Grade 9 to 12.
    Includes bibliographical references and index.
    ISBN 978-1-4677-6148-2 (lb : alk. paper) – ISBN 978-1-4677-9576-0 (eb pdf)
    1. Doping in sports–Juvenile literature. I. Title.
 RC1230.M39 2016
    362.29'088796–dc23   2015016192

Manufactured in the United States of America
1 – VP – 12/31/15

CONTENTS

CHAPTER ONE
THE PRICE OF
VICTORY

Excitement rippled through the crowd as the cyclists came into view. Almost five hundred thousand people, many from the United States, had come to see the finish of the 1999 Tour de France, the world's most famous bicycle race. Pedaling furiously, the cyclists roared past at more than 25 miles (40 kilometers) per hour. Covering more than 2,000 miles (3,200 km), much of it across rugged and steep terrain in the French Alps, the grueling race challenges the stamina, physical strength, and determination of each of the hundreds of competitors.

After three weeks on the road, the cyclists at the 1999 event were both exhausted by their ordeal and energized by the excitement of the moment. Once the competitors crossed the finish line, the outcome became official: Lance Armstrong of the US Postal Service team had won the prestigious race. His victory would propel the sport from relative obscurity into international prominence and secure his own place in history.

Armstrong, a cancer survivor, would go on to win six more Tour de France titles in a row. By 2005 he had become an international hero, a sought-after public speaker, and a prominent spokesperson for a variety of products, earning up to $20 million from endorsement deals and prize money each year. The Livestrong Foundation, a cancer charity he founded in 1997 as the Lance Armstrong Foundation, pulled in millions of dollars in annual donations. But even as Armstrong's celebrity skyrocketed, cracks emerged in his facade. Suspicions arose that his victories were not based on training and hard work alone. Some cycling insiders speculated that doping—the use of performance-enhancing drugs (PEDs)—played a significant role in his triumphs.

After years of denying these charges, Armstrong was finally implicated by several of his own teammates, who publicly declared that they had seen Armstrong dope and that Armstrong had pressured them to do the same. In the face of mounting evidence and legal action against him, Armstrong finally admitted in 2013 that he had indeed been using PEDs for years. As a result of his admission of guilt, the International Cycling Union (UCI), the governing body for competitive cycling, stripped Armstrong of his Tour de France titles, banned him from competitive cycling, and ordered him to return more than $3 million in prize money. Armstrong lost the respect of millions of cycling fans as well as many of the financial benefits tied to his reputation.

Yet Armstrong maintained that his actions were far from unique. While acknowledging that he had used banned substances to boost his performance, he said, "I didn't invent the [doping] culture, but I didn't try to stop it." In a 2015 interview, Armstrong emphasized that he hadn't doped in a vacuum. He maintained that his teammates, as well as the UCI, had been complicit. Armstrong was only one of many top cyclists who felt that doping was the only way to stay competitive. Continued success offered increasingly powerful incentives for doping, while the UCI turned a blind eye. Speaking about doping in the cycling world, Armstrong said, "This wave that we were all riding—the sport, the industry, the team, my [cancer] foundation, the entire cancer community—this wave was a monster."

During the peak of his career, from 1999 to 2005, Lance Armstrong helped turn the multimillion-dollar sport of competitive cycling into an international phenomenon, drawing avid fans from around the world, even as he used banned performance enhancers behind the scenes.

AN INTERNATIONAL CRISIS

Armstrong's case is one of the best-known doping scandals, but his situation is not uncommon. Scandals involving the use of PEDs have erupted periodically in every major sport, including professional baseball, football, soccer, and boxing. The Olympic Games have weathered numerous cases of doping. During or after the 2014 Sochi Winter Olympics, for example, eight athletes—the largest number since testing began in the 1960s—were disqualified for using banned substances. Throughout the world, Olympic athletes, coaches, trainers, and even sports officials have participated in widespread organized doping. According to Yevgeniya Pecherina, a former Olympic discus thrower, "99 percent of athletes selected to represent Russia [in the Olympics] use banned substances. You can get absolutely everything. Everything the athlete wants."

The prospect of being caught looms over athletes as an ever-present threat, as does the possibility of serious health consequences, including death. But athletes who decide to dope are more interested in how the drugs can help them win than in potential adverse effects. Many PEDs, including steroids and hormones, have legitimate medical uses. But athletes can also use them to enlarge muscles or to increase the oxygen supply in blood. These off-label uses can lead to enhanced speed and endurance— key advantages in endurance sports such as running, cycling, or swimming. Drugs can also help athletes deal with pain, lose weight, and mask the use of other banned substances.

All these factors improve an athlete's odds of victory. After years of rigorous training, elite athletes—those competing at the highest levels, such as the Olympics or world championships— are driven to win. A gold medal, a first-place finish, or a team championship can mean more than fame and glory. For professional players, these honors also bring multimillion-dollar salaries, and successful athletes can earn millions more in lucrative endorsement deals even after retiring from competition.

DOPING FAR FROM THE TOP

It's not just elite athletes who dope. Semiprofessionals and amateurs as young as early teens have been caught using illegal substances to boost their results. Between January and June of 2015, for example, twenty-six American minor-league baseball players were suspended after testing positive for PEDs. And amateur athletes can become just as obsessed with winning as the pros. A 2015 UCI investigation suggested that many amateur cyclists use the same types of PEDs that professionals do. British professional cyclist Joe Papp discovered this in 2006 when he began selling banned substances over the Internet. Before he was caught about a year later, Papp made more than $80,000 from buyers in North America, Europe, and Australia. Three-quarters of his customers were amateurs (mostly cyclists). Their drive to excel made a strong impression on Papp. "It is crazy that people are willing to put these dangerous pharmaceuticals into their body when there's nothing at stake," he reflected. Yet something may

THE GOLDMAN DILEMMA

In a landmark survey by Dr. Robert Goldman in the 1970s, elite athletes were asked if they would theoretically ingest an undetectable drug that guaranteed continuous sports successes for five years, followed by instant death. Fifty percent said they would take such a bargain. Repeating the survey every two years over a period of fifteen years, Goldman found little change in the percentage. However, a study published in the *British Journal of Sports Medicine* (*BJSM*) in 2013 tells a different story. The same hypothetical choice was presented to 212 participants in an elite track-and-field match in North America. Only two athletes, or 1 percent, said they would dope to win and then accept the lethal consequences. That number rose to twenty-five, or 12 percent, when the death sentence was removed. While many advocates of clean sports hope the new figures reflect a changed attitude toward doping, others suspect that anti-doping crackdowns caused some athletes to answer the question more cautiously. Health psychologist Jason Mazanov refers to a code of silence maintained by those involved in doping. "Nobody has seen anything, nobody knows anything," he says of the atmosphere. "I think that is what the athletes are reflecting [in their survey responses]."

be at stake after all, according to science writer and former pro cyclist Michael Shermer. He believes that prestige and celebrity—what he calls "bragging rights"—provide as much incentive to win as monetary gain.

The practice of doping has filtered down to college and high school athletes, some of whom see doping as a way to secure a future in professional sports. A 2012 investigation by the Associated Press (AP), which reviewed ten years of US college football rosters, revealed that thousands of players gained a great deal of weight during their first year of college. "It's not brain surgery to figure out what's going on," said anti-doping researcher Don Catlin on whether these players used steroids to bulk up. "To me, it's very clear." Eddie Cardieri, a former head baseball coach at the University of South Florida, expressed similar suspicions about doping in college baseball, where testing programs tend to be several steps behind the newest doping technology. "Let's face it—if players know they're not testing for a certain substance, they're more apt to [use that substance]," Cardieri stated in 2009. "The goal of all the college players is to get to the big leagues," he added, "and it becomes a vicious cycle. Kids playing in college are seeing results of these major league players and are saying, 'I gotta be like those guys.'"

"IF THE GOAL IS TO PROTECT HEALTH"

The desire to hit more home runs, score more touchdowns, or shave critical seconds off track and swim speeds is familiar to any competitive athlete. High salaries for professional athletes and the lucrative endorsement deals that accompany high-profile victories can be strong motivators. Despite the risks to athletes' reputations and health, the incentives and pressure to use PEDs remain intense. "I felt like I had all the weight of the world on top of me," explained Major League Baseball (MLB) player Alex Rodriguez in 2009 when he admitted to steroid use earlier in his career, "and I needed to perform, and perform at a high level every day. . . . I had just signed this enormous contract. . . . I felt like I needed something, a push . . . to get me to the next level."

" I FELT LIKE I HAD ALL THE WEIGHT OF THE WORLD ON TOP OF ME.

ALEX RODRIGUEZ "

To deal with the widespread use of PEDs in competitive sports around the world, some experts want to change attitudes and laws. For example, Jason Mazanov, a founding editor of the journal *Performance Enhancement and Health*, believes that the most practical way to deal with the problem is "to move on from saying 'drugs are bad' and start looking at new ways of dealing with drugs in sports." Rather than seeking to eliminate the use of PEDs, Mazanov and others suggest legalizing them so that their use can be monitored and managed for maximum safety. Supporters of this strategy argue that taking medical drugs to increase strength or stamina is little different from taking vitamins. It's a personal decision, and one the athlete should be free to make. After all, say legalization advocates, drugs will never replace the need for practice and training. They can simply become one more part of an athlete's fitness routine, like having a strict diet or following a strenuous exercise program.

Those pushing for legalization don't deny the dangers of using drugs. On the contrary, they are keenly aware that many athletes turn to underground (illegal) supplies of PEDs, which can pose even greater health risks than substances prescribed by physicians. With that in mind, some argue that legalizing doping and requiring medical supervision would make the practice much safer. "If the goal is to protect health," said Andy Miah, a bioethicist at the University of the West of Scotland, "then medically supervised doping is likely to be a better route [than banning all doping]." Doctors would monitor the athletes' health carefully, which would lower the risk of health complications. A guaranteed legal supply would mean that athletes would feel no need to resort to unsafe black market drugs, relying instead on more responsibly manufactured legal substances.

Furthermore, those who favor legalization contend that allowing athletes to dope would level the playing field. As it currently stands, athletes using PEDs have a distinct advantage over opponents who do not dope. In theory, if all athletes were free to dope without fear of getting caught, no one would have an unfair advantage over anyone else.

"AN ARMS RACE"

Those who oppose legalization of doping point out that even the best medical supervision cannot completely eliminate the safety risks athletes face if they decide to dope. Depending on the kind and amount of drugs they take, athletes may suffer liver damage, heart problems, high blood pressure, violent mood swings, baldness, sterility, or the growth of cancerous tumors. Teenage athletes may find that their growth is stunted.

Should athletes have the right to take such risks in an effort to boost their stamina? Supporters of doping regulations say no. They contend that the dangers of even medically prescribed and

DOES DOPING ALWAYS WORK?

A 2015 study suggests that doping may not always give athletes the competitive edge they seek. Sometimes doping may actually hinder the athlete's performance. Researchers came to this conclusion after comparing Olympic scores from different historical periods. Scores from events that took place after doping became common were expected to reflect a higher level of achievement than scores from earlier Olympics, but this was not the case. Although some athletes may experience improvement when doping, the authors of the study believe that the physical benefits of doping have been overrated. They concluded, "Doping may produce a minor improvement in one aspect of performance, but in other areas it may have a detrimental effect, which outweighs the positive." They expressed the hope that their findings will "help stamp out doping in sport."

monitored PEDs outweigh any possible benefits. Moreover, anti-doping advocates say that instead of leveling the playing field, legalization would put added pressure on athletes who do not want to dope. Doping would be considered mainstream, something all athletes do to maintain a competitive edge. Athletes would focus on finding the newest and most powerful supplements, rather than relying solely on their training and accepting the limits of their natural capacities. "There's an arms-race quality to performance-enhancing technologies in sport," says Thomas Murray, former head of Hastings Center, a bioethics organization in Garrison, New York. Just as nations stockpile weapons to keep pace with the supplies of other countries, athletes strive to ensure that their doping practices are on par with those of their opponents. Murray and others feel that legalizing doping would further prioritize drug use over effort and skill.

This is not the purpose of sports, say advocates of "clean" athletics. When the pressure to win becomes too great, sports are no longer enjoyable, healthy, or honest, they say. LaDonna Reed is a former track-and-field Olympian, an Olympic education specialist, and an expert on anti-doping policy. She values the way athletic competition "brings together all walks of life and all nations. . . . Even if you don't understand each other's language, a smile, high five, thumbs up, or pat on the back after a race is understood by all." From her perspective, this kind of solidarity is only possible when athletes value the challenge of the competition as much as they value winning—and when they meet that challenge honestly.

An honest challenge is what Pierre de Coubertin, the founder of the modern Olympics, had in mind when he said in the early twentieth century, "The important thing in the Olympic Games is not winning but taking part. Just as in life, the aim is not to conquer but to struggle well." To keep that sentiment alive, athletes, coaches, physicians, and officials must navigate the complex world of doping that thrives beneath the surface of every sport.

CHAPTER TWO
A BRIEF HISTORY OF DOPING

The crowd thought the race was over. Fred Lorz had just crossed the Olympic marathon finish line in Saint Louis, Missouri, on August 30, 1904. Still miles away, runner Thomas Hicks thought the race was over too. Weak and dehydrated, he scarcely had the strength to go on. But before Lorz could receive the gold medal, officials learned that he had violated the rules by riding 11 miles (18 km) of the hilly course in an automobile. Upon learning the news, the crowd booed, while word filtered back to Hicks and the other runners that the race was still on. Hicks's trainers had already injected him with strychnine—a highly toxic stimulant—mixed with egg whites. To increase his stamina further, they administered a second dose. But the mixture did more harm than good. A race official recalled that "[Hicks] could scarcely lift his legs, while his knees were almost stiff." Hicks became mentally disoriented. While he shuffled his feet, his trainers had to carry him over the finish line.

Hicks won the marathon, but at a steep price. During the race, he lost 8 pounds (3.6 kilograms). For an hour afterward, he was too ill to move. When he finally recovered, he made no secret about having used strychnine for the race. But unlike Lorz's automobile ride, this first known instance of doping in the modern Olympics was not considered cheating. In fact, US sports expert Charles Lucas hailed Hicks as a patriot "kept in mechanical action by the use of drugs, that he might bring America the Marathon honors." Lucas added that the race proved "drugs are of much benefit to athletes."

A COMPETITIVE EDGE

Lucas's thinking was very much in line with accepted views of the time. In fact, throughout the history of sports, athletes have ingested substances to gain an advantage over competitors. As early as 1700 BCE, ancient Greek athletes regularly ingested bull or sheep testicles—which contain large amounts of the hormone testosterone—to boost their strength and speed. Roman gladiators around the first century CE used stimulants such as strychnine to overcome exhaustion and increase strength. For thousands of years, few athletes or spectators questioned such strategies. In the early twentieth century, coaches and teams often created and openly advertised their own performance-enhancing concoctions with ingredients such as cocaine, heroin, strychnine, and caffeine.

PEDs became even more widespread with the introduction of anabolic steroids, which are drugs that increase muscle mass and strength. A Swiss pharmaceutical company synthesized an early anabolic steroid, Dianabol, in the 1950s, but an American, Dr. John Bosley Ziegler, is generally credited with the drug's popularity. An enthusiastic bodybuilder, Ziegler was the team physician of the York Barbell Club, an organization for weight lifters in New Jersey. Starting in 1959, he provided Dianabol to weight lifters in his club. Their improvement was swift and dramatic. As word of the new synthetic compound spread, weight lifters from other organizations and other parts of the country began demanding Dianabol. Some of them went on to become coaches in other sports and promoted

Bodybuilder Arnold Schwarzenegger, shown here at a 1974 competition, acknowledged in 1977 that he and other professional bodybuilders used steroids to boost muscle mass.

the use of anabolic steroids throughout the United States. While Ziegler had been very careful to prescribe what he considered safe doses of Dianabol, many athletes chose to exceed those amounts. Appalled by escalating usage, Ziegler eventually turned against the drug he'd once promoted. "It's a disgrace," he lamented shortly before his death in 1983. "Who plays sports for fun anymore?"

Indeed, fun was not the driving force in the highest levels of athletics during the second half of the twentieth century. Starting in the 1950s, the Cold War—a period of intense political, economic, and social rivalry between the United States and the Soviet Union (fifteen republics that included Russia) that lasted from 1945 until the collapse of the Soviet Union in 1991—heightened the two nations' competitiveness at international sporting events. Leaders on both sides wanted to prove that their athletes were stronger and better prepared. In view of the political stakes, some coaches, athletes, and sports authorities considered doping justified if it helped to uphold the United States' world standing.

THE EAST GERMAN DOPING CONSPIRACY

From the 1960s through the late 1980s, East Germany staked much of its world prestige on athletics. A government-sponsored doping program forced about ten thousand athletes with Olympic potential—some as young as eleven—to ingest steroids. "We were vehicles to prove that socialism was better than capitalism," recalled former swimming champion Carola Beraktschjan, referring to the contrasting government and economic systems of the Soviet Union and the United States. "What happened to our bodies was entirely secondary to that political mission."

The true extent of the East German doping tradition did not come to light until after the fall of communism in East Germany in 1989. Werner Franke, a world-renowned biochemist, and his wife, Brigitte Berendonk, a former Olympic discus thrower, spent years researching the medical records of former East German Olympians. Berendonk's 1991 book revealed their findings, including their belief that the doping program continued even after the fall of communism.

Many top athletes hadn't even been aware that they were taking PEDs. Angered at the deception, Ines Schmidt Geipel, who helped set a relay record in 1984, asked to have her name removed from the record books. "They gave me those drugs and lied about what they were," she declared, "and in doing so they robbed me of who I was, and who I am. I believe that I could have been a champion without steroids. . . . But I will never know, no one will ever know, because they robbed me of the chance to find out what my true potential was."

With their countries' reputations on the line, some athletes and coaches in both nations were willing to do whatever it took to win.

OLYMPIC DOPING SCANDAL

During the 1960 Olympic Games in Rome, twenty-three-year-old Danish cyclist Knud Jensen fell off his bicycle, fractured his skull, and died. At first, the emergency responders blamed his death on heatstroke, but the weather had been fairly mild. Two other Danish cyclists had also collapsed, and the director of the hospital treating them wondered why only Danish athletes were stricken. An autopsy showed that Jensen had ingested Ronicol, a drug that stimulates blood flow, as well as a variety of amphetamines that affected his heart and nervous system. Officials on the International Olympic Committee (IOC), the organization that oversees the Olympic Games, expressed shock. Conveniently forgetting some previous incidents of a similar nature, the IOC's then president Avery Brundage insisted, "I've been connected with sports for sixty years, and I've never considered such a thing."

Jensen's death made it impossible for the IOC to continue ignoring the use of PEDs. Four years later, the IOC took a stronger stance against doping after a medical report on the 1964 Tokyo Summer Olympics revealed that "certain athletes had been given shots and . . . some teams had drugs and artificial stimulants with them." IOC officials declared that in the future, doping athletes and teams could be disqualified from the games.

The year 1968 marked the first time in history that selected Olympic athletes were required to submit to tests for a variety of drugs, stimulants, and alcohol. Out of more than seven hundred tests performed at that year's Winter Games in Grenoble, France, and the 1970 Summer Games in Mexico City, only one person was found to have ingested a banned substance. Did this mean no one else was doping? Not according to Dr. Eduardo

Hay of the IOC medical commission. He noted that many of the analyzed samples contained unidentified substances with chemical makeups similar to known PEDs, but these drugs were not included on the IOC's list of banned substances. As scientists working for the IOC and other sports organizations developed new and better tests, other scientists and doctors—who stood to gain lucrative payoffs—found ways to help athletes get around them.

WHO PLAYS SPORTS FOR FUN ANYMORE?

DR. JOHN BOSLEY ZIEGLER

An anonymous US weight lifter summed up the competitive tension between dopers and enforcers at the 1968 Summer Games when he remarked, "What ban? Everyone is using a new [drug] from West Germany. They [chemists analyzing the samples] couldn't pick it up in the test they were using. When they get a test for that one, we'll find something else. It's like cops and robbers."

A turning point came at the 1988 Summer Olympics when Canadian sprinter Ben Johnson tested positive for the steroid Stanozolol. Three days after a record-breaking triumph on the track, Johnson became the first gold medalist to forfeit the honor. The IOC's then president Juan Antonio Samaranch, anxious to preserve the reputation of the games, tried to put a positive spin on the

Canadian runner Ben Johnson enjoys his victory after a record-breaking finish in the men's 100-meter final at the 1988 Olympic Games. Three days later, after Johnson tested positive for steroid use, the International Olympic Committee stripped him of his gold medal.

situation. He saw Johnson's downfall as evidence that the drug-testing program was working. "We are winning the battle against doping," he told the press.

Behind the scenes, many people disputed his optimism. One Olympics official estimated that more than half of the athletes at that year's games had used PEDs. IOC officials faced a tough challenge. They needed to draw a strict line between what was permitted and what was not, but the decision did not rest solely with the IOC. International federations for specific sports and Olympic committees in participating nations did not always agree on what substances should be banned or on how and when to administer tests. In the absence of one universal standard for dealing with dopers, some athletes managed to avoid suspicion, and many sports federation officials overlooked evidence of doping.

Summing up the results of a Canadian government investigation into Johnson's doping, Canadian judge Charles Dubin declared in 1990 that "the failure of many sports-governing bodies to treat the drug problem more seriously and to take more effective means to detect and deter the use of such drugs has . . . contributed in large measure to the extensive use of drugs by athletes."

THE STEROID ERA

The scandals at the Olympic Games were only one aspect of global doping. At the national level, professional sports from football to tennis had also become hubs of illegal substance use. In the United States, Congress took action to combat the rising use of steroids among athletes. The Anti-Drug Abuse Act of 1988 outlawed the sale of steroids except to those with legitimate medical needs. It also set penalties for sales of steroids near schools and for any sale involving underage consumers. Two years later, Congress toughened these regulations with the Anabolic Steroids Control Act of 1990. Anyone in possession of steroids—as well as anyone who supplied these drugs—was committing a crime and could face jail time. Despite the new laws, however, some US athletes continued to take risks. Between the 1980s and the first decade of the 2000s, for instance, so many Major League Baseball (MLB) players used PEDs that the period is sometimes called the steroid era of baseball. Players displayed a new level of energy, and games became more exciting, with more runs per season than at any other time in the history of the game. Notably, San Francisco Giants player Barry Bonds hit seventy-three home runs in 2001, though he had never broken fifty in previous seasons. To many observers, his unexpected success pointed directly to steroid use.

In 2005 retired MLB player Jose Canseco openly bragged about doping in his book *Juiced: Wild Times, Rampant 'Roids, Smash Hits, and How Baseball Got Big*. "Steroids are here to stay," he predicted. "That's a fact. I guarantee it. Steroids are the future." He called himself "the godfather of steroids," claiming that steroids could be used safely and that he had showed other players how to use both steroids and growth hormones. "Steroid-enhanced athletes hit more home runs," he emphasized. "So yes, I have personally reshaped the game of baseball through my example and my teaching."

The same year Canseco's book was published, MLB team owners and players responded to a growing public outcry by agreeing to implement strict sanctions for doping. A first offense would result in a fifty-game suspension, while a second offense carried a one-hundred-game suspension. If a player was found taking steroids a third time, he would be banned from MLB for life. Even with these stiff penalties in place, officials still wanted to get to the root of the problem. MLB officials asked former US senator George J. Mitchell of Maine to investigate the past use of steroids in baseball. Mitchell, once a contender for commissioner of Major League Baseball, interviewed hundreds of people from all thirty MLB teams. The report he issued in 2007 named dozens of players who had used PEDs. Those involved "range from players whose major league careers were brief to potential members of the Baseball Hall of Fame," Mitchell reported. "They include both pitchers and position players, and their backgrounds are as diverse as those of all major league players." The responsibility for these abuses, Mitchell concluded, rested not only with individual players but with coaches, team doctors, and even baseball's top officials. "There was a collective failure to recognize the problem as it

Major League Baseball player Jose Canseco takes a swing during the 1998 American League playoffs. Canseco later wrote about his long-term use of steroids and named other MLB players who he claimed had also relied on PEDs.

emerged and to deal with it early on," he wrote. Mitchell blamed this lack of oversight and regulation for the growing use of PEDs, not only in professional athletics but among young people who imitated their heroes in the major leagues.

A WORLDWIDE ANTI-DOPING AGENCY

Baseball was just one of many sports that developed a doping culture its governing body failed to control. Athletic leagues and federations in various individual nations—and even international federations—could only do so much to regulate substance abuse among athletes. For one thing, these organizations had other priorities besides enforcing anti-doping policies. Moreover, some league and federation officials kept silent about offenders in an effort to preserve a sport's reputation. While the IOC made strides in monitoring Olympians, at the end of the twentieth century the international community had no unified anti-doping organization to monitor sporting events other than the Olympic Games.

> **STEROIDS ARE HERE TO STAY. THAT'S A FACT. I GUARANTEE IT.**
>
> JOSE CANSECO

That changed after a scandal broke just before the 1998 Tour de France. Customs officials at the French-Belgian border stopped a car belonging to the highly rated Festina cycling team and discovered four hundred vials filled with banned PEDs. Coverage of the incident drew the attention of the IOC's then president, Juan Antonio Samaranch, who believed the Festina cyclists were victims of overly strict regulations. Samaranch commented that only drugs that harmed an athlete's health should be banned—while other illegal drugs should be removed from the IOC's list of prohibited substances. Public reaction to this comment was swift and disapproving, forcing Samaranch to withdraw his controversial statement. But the damage had already been done. Samaranch's remark raised questions about the IOC's commitment to clean athletics. Even Belgium's Prince Alexandre de Mérode, head of the Olympic medical commission, concluded that "the people who want to reduce the list [of prohibited drugs] are the people who want to let doping function."

Members of the IOC were anxious to restore the institution's credibility as an enforcer of clean athletic competitions. At an emergency meeting in August 1998, IOC official Dick Pound made a bold recommendation: the IOC should establish an independent anti-doping agency with power to monitor sports organizations throughout the world. In February 1999, the IOC convened the World Conference on Doping in Sport, which included representatives from the United Nations—an international organization of nearly two hundred cooperating governments—as well as national governments from around the world. Participants agreed to support the new World Anti-Doping Agency (WADA). The IOC pledged $25 million to get the organization up and running.

The task facing WADA would be enormous. A huge underground industry supported doping, and new performance-enhancing substances and techniques were rapidly emerging on the market. At the same time, sports officials representing a wide range of nations and sports vehemently disagreed with one another about which substances should be banned and which should not. It would be up to WADA to coordinate with other sports organizations to outpace those determined to beat the system.

CHAPTER THREE
ANTI-DOPING ENFORCEMENT

Canadian cross-country skier Beckie Scott began her involvement with the anti-doping movement in 2003, when she disputed her third-place finish in the 2002 Olympic 5-kilometer event. She believed she had in fact earned first place because the top two finishers each failed a doping test related to another Olympic event. Scott cited the failed tests as evidence of continuous use of PEDs that would have affected her rivals' performances in the 5-kilometer race as well. She appealed to the Court of Arbitration for Sport (CAS), an international athletics tribunal with the authority to handle doping cases. In an Olympic first, CAS awarded Scott the gold medal and stripped the other two athletes of their medals.

Scott went on to serve in several positions with WADA, advancing to the executive committee in September 2012. "I'm the only former athlete sitting at the table, so I'll bring that perspective and that position. I still want to protect the efforts of clean athletes."

At a 2004 ceremony, Olympic skier Beckie Scott received the gold medal for a 2002 Olympic race in which she originally finished third. After the two skiers who placed ahead of her failed drug tests, Scott successfully appealed her standing in the race.

THE WADA CODE

Since the creation of WADA in 1999, the agency's members have worked hard to establish clear anti-doping policies. After considering input from all interested parties, WADA's members drafted a code that identifies unacceptable substances and techniques, spelling out penalties for users. In March 2003, at the World Conference on Doping in Sport in Copenhagen, Denmark, more than one thousand representatives of sports federations and world governments voted to accept the code. Organizations endorsing the code pledge to abide by WADA's Prohibited Substances and Methods List and its rules for dealing with athletes caught using PEDs. The code also regulates testing procedures and laboratories and provides a means for athletes with medical conditions to request exemptions from testing. Participating sports organizations, including national Olympic committees and sports federations, are required to make rules that are consistent with WADA's standards. Most groups began abiding by the code before the Athens Summer Olympic Games in 2004.

John Fahey (*right*), president of the World Anti-Doping Agency (WADA), and David Howman, the organization's director general (*left*), attend a 2008 meeting at the Olympic Museum in Lausanne, Switzerland. WADA works to ensure consistency in rules about PED use in sports around the world.

Ever since the first list was issued in 2003, WADA experts do an annual review to ensure the most recently developed PEDs and techniques are included. Occasionally substances are dropped from the list. For example, caffeine was removed from the banned category in 2004—and was returned to that category six years later. Despite the popularity of caffeine-rich substances such as coffee and chocolate, experts decided that a high level of caffeine—which can increase alertness, improve muscle contractions, and boost metabolism—could give an athlete an unfair advantage over competitors. It's up to individual athletes and their coaches to keep up to date with annual changes and to monitor the ingredients in any nutritional supplements or medications prescribed to them. Accidentally ingesting a banned substance is not considered a valid excuse by WADA or any of the agencies or federations that have pledged to uphold WADA's standards and prohibitions.

BEYOND WADA

Although WADA issues the list of banned substances, sets protocols, and approves laboratories that perform drug tests and conduct anti-doping research, it does little actual testing of athletes to detect PED use. Most doping tests are done by national and international federations that oversee individual sports. Many countries also have National Anti-Doping Organizations (collectively called NADOs)—such as the United States Anti-Doping Agency (USADA), which was established in 2000. Besides testing athletes in and out of competition, these independent organizations handle penalties for violations of the WADA code and promote anti-doping education. These roles can also be filled by Regional Anti-Doping Organizations (RADOs) that combine resources in five different areas of the world: Africa, the Americas, Asia, Europe, and Oceania.

Each year, the USADA administers thousands of annual blood and urine tests to US Olympic team members, to those seeking to qualify for the Olympics, and to athletes competing in the Pan American Games. USADA jurisdiction does not extend to other highly visible areas of athletics, such as professional baseball or football. For these and most other professional American sports, national sports federations manage their own systems of anti-doping measures.

"THE RIGHT THING TO DO"

Some sports, such as mixed martial arts (MMA) and boxing, are beyond the reach of WADA and national federations. State commissions, many of which don't conduct tests for PEDs, oversee these sports. Even when tests are performed, commissions typically announce the dates ahead of time, giving athletes a chance to mask any use of performance enhancers. This can be especially dangerous in combat sports, where an athlete using PEDs might seriously injure an opponent who is fighting clean.

Fans and athletes alike have grown concerned about the

situation. In 2009 champion boxers Floyd Mayweather Jr. and Manny Pacquiao were in negotiations to face off in a highly anticipated match, but Mayweather had concerns that Pacquiao was using steroids. Boxing has no national governing body to enforce anti-doping rules, so Mayweather asked the USADA to step in and monitor both boxers for signs of doping. "I never officially came out and said that I believe Manny Pacquiao is on steroids or that I believe he's on enhancement drugs," Mayweather clarified in 2011. "I didn't say, 'I know you doing this' or 'I know you doing that' . . . it's just my opinion." Mayweather and Pacquiao could not agree on anti-doping protocols, so their 2009 match was scrapped. (Pacquiao sued Mayweather late in 2009 for defamation over Mayweather's hints that Pacquaio was doping.) However, Mayweather arranged for the USADA to conduct drug tests before his fight with Shane Mosley in May 2010, and he continued to rely on the agency for future bouts. "Win, lose, or draw, whoever I fight still has to be tested with random blood and urine tests," Mayweather insisted.

Others involved in boxing and similar sports share Mayweather's priorities. In a further effort to promote fairness and safety in the martial arts, Margaret Goodman, a former boxing ring physician, founded the Voluntary Anti-Doping Association (VADA) late in 2011. Within two years, over fifty boxing and MMA competitors had expressed interest in joining VADA, which relies on WADA-approved labs to do its testing. Other martial arts organizations, including the Ultimate Fighting Championship (UFC), have followed Mayweather's example by paying USADA to run drug-testing programs for their athletes. "Unfortunately [state boxing commissions] are not doing the job they need to," said USADA president Travis Tygart in 2015. "If they were, fighters wouldn't be coming to us to have a robust program put in place. They wouldn't be [relying on USADA testing] if they felt confident in what was there."

For some athletes, a personal commitment to drug testing and clean fighting has paid off. By 2015 a Pacquiao-versus-Mayweather fight was on the table again. This time, both boxers agreed to submit to random drug tests overseen by the USADA. (Nonetheless, other questions of character—particularly Mayweather's history of domestic violence, for which he had faced repeated criminal charges since 2001—cast a shadow over the proceedings.) After testing clean for PEDs, the two legendary fighters finally squared off in a widely watched bout on May 4, 2015. Mayweather comfortably defeated Pacquiao—who later blamed USADA regulations for his loss, noting that he'd been struggling with a shoulder injury and that the USADA had denied his request to use a painkiller. Despite Pacquiao's criticism, Tygart hailed the boxers' anti-doping agreement as "a pretty easy program to put in place. And it's absolutely the right thing to do."

Boxer Manny Pacquiao practices for his 2015 fight against rival Floyd Mayweather. In preparation for the face-off, which carried a record-setting $300 million prize for the winner, Pacquiao and Mayweather adhered to a strict drug-testing program to ensure a clean fight.

THE COLLEGE SCENE

Anti-doping organizations for professional athletes have no control over a large slice of the doping scene: college athletics. The National Collegiate Athletic Association (NCAA) has been testing college athletes for PEDs since 1986 but has no authority to dictate policy to colleges. It's up to each school to decide what kind of testing program to implement—or whether to allow tests at all. According to an AP survey of seventy-six universities in 2011, policies vary widely among colleges. For example, at the University of Miami in Florida, an athlete caught using steroids must sit out at least half the games of the season. By contrast, the University of California, Los Angeles (UCLA), will only suspend an athlete after three failed drug tests. Some schools focus their resources on detecting athletes' use of recreational drugs such as marijuana, placing little emphasis on testing for PEDs. These inconsistent policies can make for an uneven contest on the court or field. A college football team in which steroid use is not tolerated may face a rival team in which some players rely on PEDs to make them stronger players.

Because only a small percentage of college athletes are tested and because athletes often know about tests ahead of time, very few college athletes ever test positive for PEDs, making the full extent of the doping scene impossible to track. But a number of factors point to significant steroid use in college sports, especially football, where rapid, significant weight gains among thousands of players have aroused suspicion. "Everybody knows when testing is coming," said anti-doping researcher Don Catlin in 2012. "[The players] all know. And they know how to beat the test." Players who make it to the National Football Leagues (NFL), however, may find that the system catches up with them there. According to a 2012 AP report, at least eleven players who gained large amounts of weight in college and went on to professional careers eventually failed NFL drug tests.

VITAL PARTNERSHIP

As manufacturers of medical drugs that can be abused by athletes, the pharmaceutical industry can be either a powerful ally or a source of troublesome loopholes in the fight against doping. Pharmaceutical companies often stand accused of inappropriately marketing products for harmful off-label uses. Observers allege that behind the scenes, some pharmaceutical employees trying to meet unrealistically high sales goals sell drugs to black market purchasers—or even help thieves break into warehouses and steal PEDs to sell illegally. Anti-doping advocates hope the pharmaceutical industry can address these oversights and abuses to prevent drugs from getting into dopers' hands.

In January 2015, the Second International Pharmaceutical Conference, titled "New Developments for Clean Sport and Society" took place in Tokyo, Japan. Along with pharmaceutical professionals, representatives for the major anti-doping organizations attended the conference. Addressing the assembled group, WADA president Sir Craig Reedie explained the mutual benefits of a partnership between WADA and pharmaceutical companies. In addition to enhancing its own security and standards in order to cut back on illegal drug sales, the pharmaceutical industry can share information on upcoming products that dopers might use. This early alert gives WADA time to develop effective tests for such products. For its part, WADA can share knowledge about specific products that are already being abused.

"I HAVE NOTHING TO HIDE"

Drug tests can result in confusion and unfair bans if an athlete has a legitimate medical condition that requires a medication on the banned list. Swedish ice hockey player Nicklas Backstrom (*below*) had been taking an allergy medicine containing pseudoephedrine, an amphetamine, for seven years. Hours before he was to compete in the 2014 Sochi Olympics, he was summoned to a disciplinary hearing before the IOC. Because he had tested positive for a banned substance, he was not allowed to play in the game against Canada. "I have nothing to hide," said Backstrom, who had been tested one month earlier. "I feel like I haven't done anything differently than I have the last seven years." Several weeks after the Olympics, the IOC declared that Backstrom had not meant to dope, and he was awarded the silver medal his teammates had received. But he had missed his chance to compete.

DOPERS VS. TESTERS

Anti-doping efforts rely in large measure on drug testing. When testing dates are scheduled and announced ahead of time, athletes can hide PED usage relatively easily, while randomly conducted tests aim to catch more athletes off guard. Drug-testing personnel often contend with athletes who go to great lengths to miss these unscheduled tests. Before the 2006 Winter Olympics in Turin, Italy, for example, doping control officers from the IOC showed up at the training headquarters of the Austrian cross-country ski team. The officers were supposed to conduct surprise tests, but some of the athletes had gotten word of their intentions. The testing crew couldn't locate anyone to test, and the coach was nowhere to be found either. The testers did, however, discover needles and other doping-related equipment in the players' rooms. Unauthorized to confiscate incriminating evidence, the testers could only report the incident as a missed test and tell WADA officials what they had seen. They also pointed out that the skiers were staying at a hotel operated by a former coach who had been banned from the Olympics for helping athletes dope.

The episode provoked so much suspicion that WADA, in turn, notified the IOC, which then notified the Italian government. Italy is one of the few countries with criminal penalties for sports doping. Deciding to work together, IOC officials and the Italian police showed up at the hotel the night before a skiing event. Realizing they would be expected to produce samples for testing, many athletes began to drink copious amounts of water. The testers knew that this would dilute PEDs in the athletes' urine, making them difficult to detect. In a desperate attempt to conceal doping activities, one team member threw a bag of incriminating doping materials out the window. Police spotted the action and ran outdoors to retrieve the evidence.

Several of the Austrian skiers had already left the country, perhaps in anticipation of a showdown with doping officials. The IOC crew refused to give up easily and tracked them down for testing.

Meanwhile, the Austrian Olympic Committee stepped in, criticizing its own skiing federation and questioning why athletes were involved with a banned coach in the first place. The findings led to the passage of new anti-doping laws, making Austria the fourth country—after Spain, France, and Italy—to criminalize doping. Germany would follow suit in 2015.

The situation with the Austrian skiers marked the first time that the IOC had teamed up with local police to catch Olympic dopers. Was this taking the anti-doping campaign to an unwarranted extreme? Some athletes and news commentators thought so. WADA, however, hailed the partnership as another step on the path toward thwarting those who make doping possible.

COURT OF ARBITRATION FOR SPORT

Between 2012 and 2015, thirty-four Australian football players stood accused of doping. WADA officials had gathered circumstantial evidence that sports scientist Stephen Dank had injected players with a prohibited protein in 2012. WADA's legal team first presented its case to an anti-doping tribunal run by the Australian Football League, which cleared the players of any wrongdoing in March 2015. However, WADA then appealed the decision to the highest authority in international athletics, the CAS, which agreed to hear the case in November 2015.

Established by the International Olympic Committee in 1983 and run as an independent institution since 1994, CAS can handle any dispute relating to sports, including doping cases, and hears about 350 cases per year. WADA can appeal to CAS to dispute the ruling of a national sports governing body or of a national sports arbitration association. Athletes who believe they have been banned unjustly can also appeal sanctions through CAS. Unlike traditional courts, whose authority comes from a government, CAS relies on both parties agreeing ahead of time to abide by its decision. Based in Lausanne, Switzerland, CAS also has courts in New York and in Sydney, Australia.

SPORTS GOVERNING BODIES

A variety of governing bodies monitor and enforce the rules of sports, both during and out of competition. Some governing bodies control a single sport within a specific area (such as a region or a country), while others have jurisdiction over multiple sports.

TYPE	EXAMPLES
National professional sports leagues	National Bicycle League, National Hockey League (NHL), National Football League (NFL), Association of Tennis Professionals
National federations for individual professional sports	United States Soccer Federation
National federations for multiple sports	United States Olympic Committee
International federations for individual sports	United Cyclists International (UCI), International Tennis Federation (ITF)
International federations for multiple sports	International Association of Athletics Federations (IAAF), International Olympic Committee (IOC)
National anti-doping agencies	United States Anti-Doping Agency (USADA)
International anti-doping agency	World Anti-Doping Agency (WADA)

CAS draws on more than three hundred arbitrators, or judges, from eighty-seven countries. Three arbitrators hear each case. The opposing sides each choose one arbitrator, and the International Council of Arbitration for Sport (ICAS) selects the third. Because the arbitrators are well versed in sports, cases are usually resolved more quickly and with less expense than in a civil court of law. However, because disputes can arise during the Olympics and require speedy resolution, CAS has special divisions for the Summer and Winter Olympic Games. Streamlined procedures generally allow a special division to render a decision within twenty-four hours.

GOVERNMENTS AGAINST DOPING

National governments also have a significant role to play in upholding the WADA code. To make their commitment official, representatives from almost one hundred countries worked through the United Nations Educational, Scientific and Cultural Organization (UNESCO) to draft a treaty, the International Convention against Doping in Sport, which went into effect in 2007. As of 2015, over 170 countries, including the United States, have ratified the treaty. Although this document does not give countries the power to sanction athletes, it signals their commitment to establish national drug-testing programs for their athletes; to deny funds to athletes, trainers, and doctors who violate the anti-doping code and to sports federations that ignore the code; and to fund anti-doping education. UNESCO itself shares these powers and promotes anti-doping legislation in countries that seek its aid.

Crucially, to combat the rapid development of new doping techniques and PEDs, UNESCO and the convention's partner governments raise money for scientific research to counter these advances. Between 2001 and 2015, WADA spent more than $60 million dollars to support scientists researching ways to prevent and detect doping. In 2013 Thomas Bach, president of the International Olympic

> ## WIN, LOSE, OR DRAW, WHOEVER I FIGHT STILL HAS TO BE TESTED.
>
> FLOYD MAYWEATHER

Committee, announced that the organization would donate $10 million for anti-doping research. He also asked world governments to add to the fund. China was the first nation to heed Bach's plea, contributing $1 million in September 2014. WADA president Sir Craig Reedie called China's donation "an excellent example of how sport and government can work together . . . to help give athletes the level playing field they so deserve." Bach indicated the investment would help preserve the competitive nature of athletics, saying "it is vital for the future of sport that we protect clean athletes. . . . Without clean athletes there can be no credible competition, and without credible competition sport will also cease to be attractive to spectators and fans and would ultimately wither and die."

CHAPTER FOUR
WHAT DOPERS ARE USING

Years of doping transformed Tammy Thomas's body—and not in the ways she expected or wanted. In 2013, more than ten years after she had stopped using anabolic steroids, the forty-three-year-old former champion track cyclist still felt the drugs' long-term effects. Although the most obvious side effects—masculine traits such as bulging muscles, extensive weight gain, irregular hair growth, and an Adam's apple—had faded, Thomas blamed the PEDs for a range of ongoing health problems, including chronic fatigue. As a young and impressionable athlete, she had taken substances her coach provided without suspecting they would take such a heavy toll on her body.

Thomas's experience is far from unique. Many athletes have little idea of the health risks posed by PEDs until after they become dependent on a banned substance. Negative side effects can persist for years or even a lifetime, with some health problems arising for the first time long after PED use ends.

US track cyclist Tammy Thomas, shown here after winning a race at the 2002 UCI Track Cycling World Cup, experienced numerous side effects from PED use. The steroids she ingested caused her to develop masculine physical traits as well as other health problems.

BEHIND THE BAN

While many athletes avoid PEDs, others ignore WADA's regulations, grasping for any new product or method that might give them a competitive edge. The list of substances banned by WADA regularly changes to accommodate the latest drugs and practices. Three factors determine whether a chemical compound is included on the WADA list of banned substances:

- The substance or technique must have a proven effect on physical performance.
- The substance or technique must pose a threat to the athlete's health.
- The substance or technique must be considered contrary to "the spirit of sport."

Any two of these three conditions is enough to place a substance on the banned list. Hundreds of doping substances have

The placebo effect is the power of a patient's belief that he or she has received a beneficial medicine or treatment. Even if a neutral substance, or placebo, is substituted for the real product, the patient's expectation of a benefit leads to actual improvement. The same may be true for athletes taking PEDs. A well-known example concerned Richard Virenque's performance at the 1998 Tour de France. Before one leg of the race, he wanted to try a "special" substance that members of another team had mentioned to him. Although his physiotherapist, Willy Voet, was involved with doping, he hesitated to give a totally unknown mixture to the star cyclist. But Virenque insisted, so Voet injected Virenque with a simple sugar solution instead of the unfamiliar substance. Virenque credited his excellent showing to the last-minute "performance enhancer." According to Voet, as well as some others who have studied doping, "There is no substitute for self-belief."

been identified, and more are likely to be developed and added to the list. Although some drugs are only banned during competitions, many are prohibited at all times.

Major banned performance-enhancing substances and techniques include the following:

- **Anabolic steroids** are among the most common PEDs. Steroids build muscle mass, increase strength, and accelerate recovery from an injury or from fatigue. Dopers usually take steroids orally or by injection. Sometimes the substance comes in a cream or gel form that can be rubbed into the skin.

Because the body naturally produces certain steroids, such as testosterone, a blood or urine test is considered positive if the level of steroids is higher than normal. Elevated levels of synthetically produced steroids can lead to high blood pressure, heart disease, liver disease, excessive aggression and mood swings, and infertility. Women may develop male characteristics such as facial hair and a deepening voice, in addition to facing an increased risk of birth defects for any children they might have in the future.

- **Hormones** occur naturally in the body but may seriously impair health when synthetic versions are taken in large quantities. One popular performance enhancer, **human growth hormone** (HGH) increases overall strength and promotes muscle mass. Taken in large quantities, HGH has a long list of possible side effects including anxiety, heart disease, muscle and bone pain, and cancer. Young people might experience abnormal skeletal growth. Experts estimate that some dopers may be taking ten times the amount of a normal medical dose of HGH, greatly magnifying their risk.

- **Beta2-agonists** are common treatments for patients with asthma. Usually inhaled in the form of an aerosol or a dry powder, they open up air passages and increase the flow of oxygen. This improved respiration can increase endurance. Possible side effects include headaches, nausea, muscle cramps, and an irregular heartbeat.

- **Stimulants**, from caffeine to amphetamines, boost energy and increase alertness. Among the many possible side effects are high blood pressure, an irregular heart rhythm, and increased risk of heart attack or stroke. Although stimulants are banned during actual competitions, they are not prohibited at all times. Because many are sold over the counter and are widely used by the general population, WADA has tried to build some leeway into its testing program for stimulants. If the measurement of certain stimulants is below a certain level, the athlete is not considered to be doping.

BLOOD DOPING

Some athletes try to improve their endurance by increasing the number of red blood cells in their blood. Known as blood doping, this practice often involves injecting the hormone *erythropoietin* (EPO), which stimulates increased production of red blood cells, boosting stamina and endurance—though at great risk. A large quantity of extra red blood cells can thicken the blood and lead to blood clots, heart attacks, and strokes. One of the most dangerous doping substances, EPO is believed to have caused the deaths of twenty European cyclists between 1987 and 2007.

Another method of blood doping consists of a transfusion from a matched blood donor or from the athlete's own body. In the latter case, the athlete can extract some of his or her own blood using a syringe and a blood bag, then refrigerate the blood for weeks or even months. This loss of blood prompts the body to make more red blood cells. After the athlete's red blood cell count returns to normal naturally, he or she can then receive a transfusion of the stored blood, producing a much higher red cell count than normal and boosting the oxygen content in the blood. Although this form of blood doping does not involve ingesting a foreign substance, athletes who dope this way are manipulating their bodies in a way that gives them an unfair advantage over clean athletes. For this reason, manipulated blood transfusions are considered a form of cheating.

GENE DOPING

One potential form of bodily manipulation is, in some ways, still closer to science fiction than fact. Gene therapy, the insertion of

In medical settings and in laboratories such as this one, blood samples are often stored in blood bags. Using similar equipment, athletes who practice blood doping often draw and store their own blood in their homes or in hotel rooms. They later transfuse this blood back into their bodies to boost their red blood cell count.

certain genes into patients' cells, may eventually lead to medical breakthroughs in treating a wide variety of conditions, including cancer, blood diseases, and muscle degeneration. Practical medical use of this method is still in its infancy and carries great risks, but that is unlikely to deter athletes and coaches seeking new performance-enhancement options. The idea of injecting genes that promote muscle growth, speed, and stamina appeals to many would-be dopers—especially because such genetic changes are difficult to detect through current doping tests. As early as 1994, Olympic officials were discussing "how to prevent genetic manipulation and thwart the maneuvers of those scientists who

SCIENTISTS ON THE SPOT

As French gene therapy researcher Philippe Moullier discovered, many would-be dopers are willing to try even the newest, most unpredictable scientific advancements in the hope of staying one step ahead of testing agencies. Moullier's team of scientists discovered that the gene for the hormone EPO—coveted by doping athletes for its production of red blood cells—can be artificially created in a lab. Soon after he and his team announced their findings in 2008, several ex-professional cyclists visited Moullier's lab. Claiming to be members of an anti-doping group, they wanted to learn more about his work. At first, Moullier was happy to talk with them about both the promise and the dangers of the synthetic EPO gene. He explained that introducing an artificial EPO gene into a person's body could trigger a massive overproduction of red blood cells that might lead to blood clots or make the blood too thick to flow easily. But to Moullier's surprise, his visitors showed no interest in the medical repercussions. He began to suspect that they were more interested in tapping into EPO's performance-enhancing potential than in fighting doping. "The competition is so high," Moullier later remarked, "those guys [elite athletes] are ready to do anything to make the difference"—even using experimental substances with unpredictable, potentially life-threatening effects.

work for doping." Despite their efforts, dopers continue to seek out this developing technology.

The first publicized instance of attempted gene doping involved a gene therapy called Repoxygen. Originally developed in a British pharmaceutical lab in 2002, Repoxygen (since

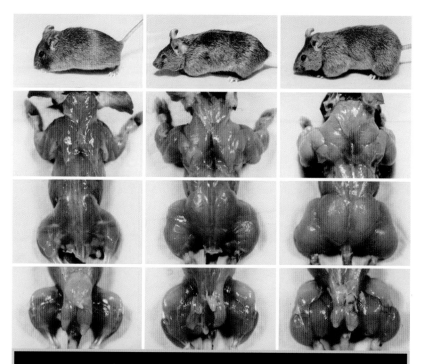

Experiments with mice have shown that genetic manipulation can significantly affect muscle mass, speed, and other traits. The mouse shown in the first column at left of this chart is a typical mouse with no changes to its genes. The mice in the second and third columns have been genetically altered.

discontinued) was intended to increase red blood cells in patients with anemia, a condition involving a shortage of red blood cells. German track coach Thomas Springstein had different ideas for the product. In 2004 law enforcement officials, investigating him on other doping charges, came across a suspicious e-mail he had sent to a doctor working for a Dutch speed skating team. "The new Repoxygen is hard to get," wrote Springstein. "Please give me new instructions soon so that I can order the product before Christmas." These words made headlines during his

THE LAST WISH OF
LYLE ALZADO

One of the strongest voices against doping in the late twentieth century came from former National Football League (NFL) player Lyle Alzado. In 1991, the year before his death from brain cancer at the age of forty-three, Alzado spoke out against steroid use in a widely read issue of *Sports Illustrated* magazine. While admitting there was no conclusive proof of a connection, Alzado blamed his brain cancer on the massive amount of steroids he used for more than fourteen years. He hoped to save other players from a similar fate. "Ninety percent of the athletes I know are on the stuff [steroids]," he wrote. "We are not born to be 300 pounds [136 kg] or jump thirty feet [9 m]. All the time I was taking steroids, I knew they were making me play better. But I became very violent on the field and off it. . . . Now look at me. My hair is gone. I wobble when I walk and I have to hold on to someone for support. I have trouble remembering things. My last wish? No one should ever die this way."

doping trial in 2006, and the sports world immediately took an interest in Repoxygen. Though investigators found no evidence that Springstein had ever actually obtained the drug, would-be dopers were intrigued. In the wake of Springstein's trial, athletes and teams contacted Repoxygen's developers, hoping for more information. Anti-doping authorities and scientists feared the publicity would spur more dopers to pursue gene doping.

Experts anticipate that gene doping will become common practice in athletics as gene therapy techniques advance. In 2014 rumors surfaced that Olympic athletes in Sochi were using a muscle-building gene therapy substance undetectable to WADA doping tests. Though no one could confirm the rumors, WADA and other sports organizations are well aware of the challenge they face. If and when athletes begin using gene doping, regulators will need new technology to test athletes. Since 2003 WADA has spent millions of dollars to fund research into appropriate technology. The quest for reliable detection of gene therapy use has become part of the ongoing race between dopers and anti-doping agencies.

CHAPTER FIVE
BEATING THE SYSTEM

Marion Jones had no intention of getting caught using banned substances. Widely considered "the greatest female athlete in the world," the runner won three gold and two bronze medals at the 2000 Summer Olympics in Sydney, Australia. Around the same time, she began using a new illegal anabolic steroid provided by her coach Trevor Graham. The new substance was appealing because blood or urine samples would test "clear" of the drugs, giving the steroid its unofficial name, The Clear.

In 2003, USADA received a mysterious syringe containing trace amounts of The Clear. The sample came from an anonymous tipster—eventually discovered to be Graham—who claimed that the Bay Area Laboratory Co-operative (BALCO), a San Francisco nutritional supplement company already under government scrutiny, was distributing the illegal drug. Although Graham would later deny any involvement in doping and insist he "was just a coach doing the right thing," investigators determined that he had purchased The Clear from BALCO and had provided it to the Olympic runners he trained. While a team of scientists at

World-famous runner Marion Jones competes in the women's 200-meter final at the 2000 Olympics. Jones eventually shocked fans by admitting that she had used PEDs.

the University of California, Los Angeles, worked to design a new test that could detect the substance, federal authorities launched an investigation of BALCO.

Investigators questioned dozens of prominent athletes—including Jones, who denied that she had ever used The Clear. Still, the federal investigation revealed that BALCO had sold PEDs to coaches and athletes involved in baseball, boxing, cycling, American football, and numerous Olympic sports. BALCO's owner, Victor Conte, pled guilty to distributing drugs and to fraud in a scandal that implicated coaches, trainers, and dozens of top athletes. One of those athletes was Jones, who admitted that she had lied to investigators about her use of steroids, wanting to save her career and the reputation of her coach. Because perjury—lying under oath in a courtroom—is a crime, Jones was sentenced to six months in prison. In response to her confession of cheating, the US Olympic Committee stripped her of her five Olympic medals. "This is a shame," remarked Dick Pound, then WADA's president, noting that Jones "was America's darling" and had inspired millions of fans around the world. Still, Pound emphasized his conviction that even the most revered athletes should not escape the consequences of cheating. "All the people who have been part of that system have been busted," Pound said. "You hope it's the end of the batch of bad apples and the new generation has learned from it, but we'll see."

Marion Jones's efforts to conceal her use of PEDs had failed, but the well-publicized case did not stop other athletes from attempting to cover up their doping, nor did it stop anti-doping authorities from pursuing them vigorously.

FOOLING THE TEST

For athletes relying on PEDs, finding a way to test clean is a high priority. Athletes may take steroids during training to increase the size of their muscles and to boost their strength. Then, as the date of a competition approaches, they stop taking the drugs. No trace of steroids remains in their bodies when they are tested, yet they still benefit from the gains they made during training. This method also works for the hormone EPO.

However, timing drug use for maximum benefit and minimum risk of detection isn't a foolproof technique. WADA officials know this tactic and aim to counter it with out-of-competition testing. Anti-doping agencies require athletes to report on their whereabouts in the months and weeks leading up to an event. During this period, athletes are subjected to drug testing without notice. "Our testing is now very strategic," remarked USADA president Travis Tygart in 2012.

THE BALCO SYSTEM

Sprinter Kelli White, the first athlete implicated in the 2003 BALCO drug scandal, initially denied doping, claiming that the stimulant found in her test sample was medically prescribed for narcolepsy, or sleeping sickness. Less than a year later, she came clean, admitting she'd purchased PEDs from BALCO's owner, Victor Conte. She was banned from competition.

White then became the first athlete to ever actively work with the United States Anti-Doping Agency. In interviews and at professional conferences, she has spoken out against doping, stressing that athletes rarely dope without assistance. "I want to explain what it takes for the whole system to work," she said at a Danish conference in 2005. "[My doping] took not only Conte's help, it took my coach, making me believe it was OK. I think a lot of the time, what happens to athletes is that people make you believe that what you are doing is OK because everyone else is doing it."

Victor Conte, the owner of the Bay Area Laboratory Co-operative, showcases the nutritional supplement ZMA, which his company produced and illegally marketed to athletes.

"We have two goals—maximum deterrence and maximum detection."

When careful timing of drug use isn't enough to help athletes escape detection, dopers may try to conceal their activities by substituting someone else's "clean" sample for their own. This can be difficult because of the protocols surrounding the collection of urine samples. At the 2004 Summer Olympics in Atlanta, Georgia, for example, the IOC caught a Hungarian discus thrower trying to smuggle untainted urine into the test area. Two years later, an Olympic weight lifter from India unsuccessfully tried to evade detection by strapping a bag of clean urine to his waist under his clothes.

MASKING AGENTS

Besides timing their use of drugs so they do not show up in screenings, athletes have other ways to hide their doping—such as ingesting additional drugs. Masking agents do not enhance performance, but they camouflage other drugs, making PEDs difficult

"DOPING IS NOT AN ACCIDENT"

Perhaps no one has heard more implausible explanations for doping than former WADA president Dick Pound. In his 2006 book *Inside Dope*, he lists almost four pages of excuses for positive test results. Among these was a German runner's claim that someone had spiked his toothpaste. A cyclist from Lithuania maintained that the thirty-seven PEDs found in his wife's car really belonged to his mother-in-law. Perhaps most unconvincing of all, a British athlete insisted that the anabolic steroids found in his testing sample were the result of shampoo that he had drunk. Pound is unimpressed by such excuses. "Doping is not an accident," he emphasizes.

to detect in blood or urine samples. For this reason, WADA includes all known masking agents on its banned substance list.

Banned masking agents include the following:

- **Diuretics**, commonly used on patients with congestive heart failure, increase the production of urine. When used as a masking agent, they dilute PEDs and flush them out of the body more quickly, so a drug test will register negative. On the downside, using diuretics can cause dehydration, muscle cramps, low blood pressure, and fainting.
- **Epitestosterone** is a hormone the body naturally produces. Drug tests to determine whether an athlete has taken testosterone usually measure the testosterone level against the body's epitestosterone level. Normally the two hormones are about equally balanced in the body, but if a test shows that the amount of testosterone is much greater than that of epitestosterone, testers know that an athlete is boosting the testosterone level artificially. To mask this, a doper can also take enough epitestosterone to balance the two substances. In this case, the test will return a negative result for doping.
- **Plasma expanders** increase the blood's liquid portion, or plasma, diluting the presence of banned drugs such as EPO.
- **Secretion inhibitors** block drugs from being removed by the kidneys. A substance therefore stays in the body and is not excreted in the urine. A urine drug test will reveal nothing.

BIOLOGICAL PASSPORTS

British cyclist Jonathan Tiernan-Locke never tested positive for PEDs, and he denies ever doping. But two years after he won the 2012 Tour of Britain, UCI found him guilty of blood boosting, stripped him of his title, and imposed a two-year ban on competitions. "I'm not bitter about it," said Tiernan-Locke, who had won four stage races and seemed destined for athletic stardom. "I know I won those races fair and square, but I am still stunned by what happened."

"What happened" involves a controversial technique to detect doping: a biological passport. In 2009 WADA introduced the first type of biological passport, called the hematological module, which screens for blood doping. The biological passport is essentially a comparison technique. Instead of relying on a single test for a specific drug, professional testers take a broader perspective, tracking crucial factors in an athlete's blood samples over an extended period. Rather than look for the drug itself, analysts watch for changes in the blood that may indicate doping has taken place. This can help them detect the use of substances that would otherwise be easy to mask.

Tiernan-Locke was accused of doping based on the findings of the hematological module that monitored his red blood cell count. Red blood cells contain the protein hemoglobin, which delivers oxygen to the muscles. A high level of red blood cells gives an athlete strength and endurance. When a doping athlete uses EPO, the drug causes the body to make new red blood cells, called reticulocytes. This means the athlete will have a higher ratio of reticulocytes to mature red blood cells. The same thing also happens in blood boosting when an athlete has blood removed for later transfusion. Depleted of red blood cells, the body begins to make more, resulting in a larger-than-usual number of reticulocytes. Then, when the athlete transfuses his own blood, he will have a lower percentage of reticulocytes because of the influx of mature red blood cells that outnumber them.

As passport analysts look at blood tests taken over months or years, they get a sense of an individual's normal ratio of reticulocytes to mature red blood cells. Generally people have one hundred times as many mature cells as they do reticulocytes. If the balance is significantly altered or if one of those numbers rises or falls drastically, there's a good chance doping has occurred. No positive drug test is required to confirm the use of performance-enhancing substances or techniques. Daniel Eichner, executive director of the WADA-accredited Sports Medicine Research and Testing Laboratory in Salt Lake City, Utah, compares the biological passport to a procedure for trying to catch drivers traveling over the speed limit. "Instead of trying to catch you speeding," explains Eichner, "we measure how long it takes to get from Point A to Point B, and then calculate how fast you were going." In Tiernan-Locke's case, the biological passport showed a drastic change in blood values, which experts and officials attributed to blood doping.

"NOT A CURE-ALL"

In 2013, when Lance Armstrong publicly confessed to his years of PED use, he said that his doping regimen in the Tour de France would have been difficult to keep secret if biological passports had been available at that time. As of November 2014, twenty cyclists and thirty-six track-and-field runners had been banned from their sports based on findings from their biological passports. But the system is far from foolproof.

If testing experts notice an abrupt change in the level of an athlete's red blood cells, doping isn't the only possible explanation. A sudden increase in exercise or a change in location—specifically a change in altitude—can also affect the body's production of red blood cells. A test for PEDs in addition to reading a biological passport could settle the issue, but in most cases of athletes who have been banned so far, no follow-up tests were performed. As an athlete who has been banned based on his biological passport but who never tested positive for performance enhancers, Tiernan-Locke has reservations about the accuracy

WE HAVE TWO GOALS— MAXIMUM DETERRENCE AND MAXIMUM DETECTION.

TRAVIS TYGART, CHIEF EXECUTIVE OFFICER OF USADA **"**

of the biological passport. He believes it is "great in principle," but that it should not be presented as almost indisputable evidence of doping.

If the biological passport can be mistakenly interpreted to find an innocent athlete guilty of doping, is the opposite also true? Can it fail to catch athletes who are, in fact, doping? According to Eichner, flagrant offenders will be caught. They may be new to doping and lack sophistication in their methods, or they may be overconfident or careless about their timing. But seasoned dopers know how to keep their blood profile looking normal despite their use of performance-enhancing substances and techniques. One way to do this, according to professional cyclist and convicted doper Floyd Landis, is to take very small doses of EPO while getting a blood transfusion. The tiny amount remains in the body for a few hours and triggers the production of reticulocytes. At the same time, the mature blood cells from the transfusion keep the balance between new and mature cells consistent with the athlete's biological passport. Analysts would find no alarming discrepancies.

Officials acknowledge the limitations of biological passports. The method is "not a cure-all," says Travis Tygart, head of the

USADA. "Not yet. It's a fantastic tool when used properly. That means you've got to do urine analysis, blood analysis, you've got to collect samples and you've got to have experts who can read them. . . . From a detecting point of view, it's [just] one of the tools in the toolbox."

INVISIBLE DOPERS

On January 1, 2014, WADA introduced a second biological passport, called the steroidal module, which was designed to detect synthetic steroids in the body. Researchers are also developing a third module to monitor the body's endocrine system, which produces, stores, and releases hormones. An endocrine module could identify artificially introduced hormones such as HGH. Yet even the triple-monitoring power of blood, steroid, and endocrine modules may not be enough to thwart individuals born with a surprisingly common gene deletion—a mutation in which part of a chromosome or a sequence of deoxyribonucleic acid (DNA), the body's genetic building blocks, is missing.

In a 2008 Swedish study that was partially funded by WADA, fifty-five healthy men were injected with the banned hormone testosterone. Later, their urine was screened for the substance. Thirty-eight of the tests revealed the presence of testosterone in their subjects' urine samples. However, the remaining seventeen tests showed no signs of the hormone in the urine. These seventeen men had a gene deletion that prevented their bodies from converting testosterone into a form that can be excreted in the urine. Without the enzyme, athletes cannot excrete testosterone, so their urine tests negative for doping. Even though their use of testosterone would not be apparent to doping officials, the hormone would still boost their muscle mass, giving them an advantage in athletic competitions. Another study, published in the *British Journal of Sports Medicine* in 2009, focused on soccer

A LANDMARK LAWSUIT

In 2009 German speed skater Claudia Pechstein received a two-year ban from the International Skating Union (ISU) for blood doping. Although the Olympic gold medalist had not failed a blood test, her biological passport revealed suspicious deviations from her baseline readings before some of her events. When the Court of Arbitration for Sport upheld the ban, Pechstein refused to give up. She took the unusual step of suing ISU and the German Speed Skating Association in Germany's civil court system. A district court rejected her case, but in February 2015, a higher court overturned that ruling and agreed to hear the case. If Pechstein wins her lawsuit, experts believe that other European athletes will follow her example. The CAS would no longer have the final word in sports disputes.

players. Scientists calculated that the gene deletion that masks doping existed in up to 7 percent of the study's Hispanic subjects, 10 percent of the Caucasians, and at least 30 percent of those of Asian descent.

The fact that an individual has the gene deletion doesn't mean that he or she is doping, of course. But sports officials believe that some athletes are aware of their condition and are taking advantage of it. As a result, scientists who conducted the Swedish and British studies have recommended that athletes be genetically tested for the gene deletion. Then those with the deletion could be checked for testosterone and steroid use with the sophisticated endocrine module, rather than the standard urine test.

The biological passport approach to doping has its critics. While many people accept the use of a biological passport, some feel a passport that reveals genetic information is too great an invasion of privacy. Such genetic profiling may also be too expensive for anti-doping agencies to use regularly on large groups of people. Nevertheless, anti-doping officials will continue working to close the genetic loophole in the fight against doping.

ONGOING STRUGGLE

Athletes, coaches, and others seeking to obtain performance enhancers are always looking for new or experimental products for which no tests yet exist. But even if athletes manage to fool a test, they are not permanently safe from detection. Blood and urine samples are kept for several years. If an athlete uses a substance for which no test exists, a way to screen for it may emerge in the future. Stored samples can be tested and an athlete penalized up to ten years later. The struggle between anti-doping agencies and those who dope extends far beyond the date of any athletic event.

CHAPTER SIX
SUPPLY AND DEMAND

Like most elite athletes, Major League Baseball player Alex Rodriguez wanted to reach the pinnacle of his sport. A three-time recipient of the American League Most Valuable Player (MVP) Award, Rodriguez spent years building a reputation as a powerful infielder and a skilled batter. In 2007 he became the youngest player in the history of MLB to hit five hundred home runs. But his spectacular record was tarnished when a major drug scandal came to light in 2013. Anthony Bosch, owner of the Biogenesis of America, an anti-aging clinic in Coral Gables, Florida, was at the center of this controversy. A report in the *Miami New Times* accused Bosch of supplying illegal HGH, testosterone, and anabolic steroids to professional baseball players, Rodriguez among them. Rodriguez allegedly paid Bosch $12,000 a month for drugs and services, including "tips on how to beat MLB's drug testing."

Many hormone replacement or rejuvenation clinics, such as Biogenesis, offer relatively easy access to PEDs. Athletes who visit such clinics, have their blood drawn, and go through a physical exam may secure a doctor's prescription for steroids.

Major League Baseball player Alex Rodriguez, playing for the Texas Rangers, catches a throw to second base during a 2001 game. Rodriguez struggled to rebuild his reputation after a 2013 scandal revealed his extensive use of PEDs.

Some clinics have their own pharmacies for filling prescriptions. Otherwise an athlete may fill a clinic's prescription at a local pharmacy. Although steroids are banned in all US sports, the athlete has technically gone through legal channels to obtain them and the clinic has not violated the law. However, the Biogenesis clinic overstepped legal boundaries by supplying steroids to people—including minors—without a valid medical reason. Furthermore, Anthony Bosch wore a white coat and often referred to himself as a doctor, but he had no medical degree and no legal right to prescribe drugs of any kind to anyone. In October 2014, he pled guilty to charges that he had conspired to profit from the sale of PEDs. Four months later, in February 2015, he was sentenced to four years in prison.

As a result of the scandal, Bosch's clinic shut down and could

MAKING A COMEBACK

As the Biogenesis doping scandal came to light, Major League Baseball conducted its own investigation, which resulted in the suspensions of thirteen players, including Alex Rodriguez. Twelve players accepted the fifty-game sanction, but Rodriguez received a longer sanction because he had a longer record of doping. At first, Rodriguez protested his innocence vigorously, but he later admitted his doping to federal investigators. Despite the blot on his reputation, Alex Rodriguez was determined to make a comeback. On May 7, 2015, he surpassed baseball legend Willie Mays to claim fourth place on baseball's all-time home runs list.

no longer supply athletes with performance enhancers, but those who choose to dope can obtain drugs from a variety of sources. If an athlete doesn't visit a hormone clinic, he or she may go to a cooperating general physician to get a prescription for performance enhancers. People also purchase PEDs online from black market sellers, either for their own use or to sell in turn to fellow athletes.

PHYSICIANS AND DOPING

In his 2006 book *Inside Dope*, Dick Pound recalls asking a panel of medical ethicists what they would do if approached by a top athlete who requests anabolic steroids. Everyone on the panel replied that they would prescribe the steroids. Astounded, Pound asked how they could justify such a decision. They replied that the athlete was free to weigh the pros and cons and make his or her own choice. To these doctors, their patients' right to make decisions about their bodies takes precedence over the rules of the sport and even the law. Pound considers this reasoning to be flawed and favors stiff penalties for doctors who prescribe drugs for nonmedical reasons. Yet for many physicians, the situation is not so simple. If a patient is determined to take steroids against medical advice, a doctor may feel obligated to supply those steroids so that he or she can monitor the athlete's health. Many doctors who assist athletes in doping also have more complex incentives for doing so.

Physicians who care for prominent athletes have a strong stake in their patients' success. In the United States, this is particularly true of doctors who work for professional sports teams. The association with elite sports carries tremendous publicity and prestige that can boost physicians' own careers. In fact, in many professional sports, competition is so keen for such positions that instead of receiving a salary, doctors pay for the privilege of working with a team. Hospitals also negotiate deals to become a team's official health-care provider, securing the right to advertise an exclusive connection to a team in a way designed to impress the public. Hospitals often pay teams millions of dollars a year for this marketing advantage.

The prestige that comes with being a team's medical provider often translates into financial benefits that offset the costs of these deals. Lew Lyon, vice president of Maryland's MedStar Union Memorial Hospital, the Baltimore Ravens' official health-care provider, explains what he calls the halo effect: a rise in team doctors' reputations and a related increase in the number of regular patients who see these physicians. "Friends will call me and say, 'Can you get me in to see one of the Ravens docs?' And they're very accessible. They have private practices like other physicians."

With so much of their money and reputation linked to the team

Former NFL and Canadian Football League player John Avery is examined by a team doctor for the Toronto Argonauts during preseason training camp in 2004.

and its athletes, doctors face pressure to live up to expectations. A doctor's first responsibility is to his or her patients. But team owners, not the players themselves, decide whether to keep or fire a team physician. When a football player is injured, he should not resume playing until he is fully recovered—but if the team needs him before he is ready to return, a physician faces two choices. One option is to prescribe medication to mask the pain and get the athlete back onto the field as soon as possible. This would please team managers and owners. The other option is to put the patient's well-being before everything else, which could jeopardize both the team's performance and the doctor's position as team physician. According to doping expert Dr. Jason Mazanov, physicians often "do what we are told instead of what we are supposed to do. Instead of acting in the best interests of the athlete, we are acting in the best interest of the sporting organization." The goal of these organizations, he points out, is to win and make money. In the words of Dr. Karim Khan, editor of the *British Journal of Sports Medicine*, "You have to be prepared to be sacked for your principles."

BLACK MARKET STEROIDS

Despite the pressures and incentives physicians encounter, not all doping athletes can rely on a team doctor for doping help. Doctors in the United States know they could face prosecution for prescribing steroids without a legitimate medical need. The law may have made US doctors more hesitant to write prescriptions for athletes. But as one source of illegal substances closed off— or at least narrowed considerably—athletes found a replacement: the black market.

YOU HAVE TO BE PREPARED TO BE SACKED FOR YOUR PRINCIPLES.

DR. KARIM KHAN

Since the Anti-Drug Abuse Act of 1988 went into effect, US athletes seeking steroids without a prescription must buy directly from a foreign manufacturer or a drug dealer. For many years, labs in Mexico provided most of the illegal steroids coming into the United States. In 2005 the US Drug Enforcement Administration (DEA) crippled this source of drugs with Operation Gear Grinder. The twenty-one-month investigation led to the indictment of eight Mexican businesses that produced illegal steroids and sold them over the Internet. Officials identified more than two thousand customers—including individual users, street drug dealers, and organized crime syndicates—in dozens of US cities. Pharmacies

NO FREE PASS

Despite the DEA's best efforts, raw steroid products continue to enter the United States. When one pipeline shuts down, others take its place. In May 2015, for instance, Operation Juice Box exposed a narcotic and steroid ring operating out of Connecticut. Two months of intense electronic and wire surveillance led to the seizure of hundreds of vials of steroids and other substances that had been shipped from China. Eight individuals were arrested, including a judicial marshal, a police dispatcher, and a police sergeant involved in selling the drugs. "We follow these investigations wherever they lead us—and in this case to a police officer," said DEA special agent Michael Ferguson. "Wearing a shield does not give you a free pass to peddle this poison in our neighborhood or to our families."

along the US-Mexican border received steroids from the same source and illegally sold them directly to Americans. A DEA news release called the successful drug bust "the largest steroid enforcement operation in US history."

The era of black market steroids was far from over, however. With the major Mexican suppliers out of the way, Chinese companies stepped into the picture. These businesses, legal and unregulated in China, create raw steroid powder and kits for homemade PEDs. Underground drugmakers can order these materials and chemical mixtures over the Internet and use them to produce sellable steroids. Following the success of Gear Grinder, DEA officials targeted Chinese suppliers in Operation Raw Deal. After eighteen months of investigation, agents raided fifty-six sites in the United States over a four-day period in September 2007. They seized 500 pounds (227 kg) of steroids and 1.4 million units of steroid dosage. Some of these confiscated steroids had been mixed in medical labs, while others had been created in home basements, garages, and bathrooms—often in unsanitary conditions. In some cases, amateur steroid manufacturers had added baby oil, cooking oil, peanut oil, and even horse urine to their products to stretch their materials as far as possible.

"THE ULTIMATE RAW DEAL"

Although all steroids have the potential for serious side effects, unregulated black market drugs, such as the Mexican and Chinese steroids, often contain dangerous impurities. This is partly because the chemical processes that create the steroids can also result in unwanted by-products. Pharmaceutical companies lower the risk of such contamination by using pure raw materials and controlling the time, temperature, and conditions of the chemical reactions that create a particular product. A purification process further ensures that the final steroids are untainted. Underground steroid manufacturing lacks such safeguards. The toxic effects of black market drugs are unpredictable, but experts say they may cause kidney, liver, and nerve damage.

In announcing the Raw Deal raid that shut down makeshift steroid facilities across the country, Karen Tandy, administrator for the DEA, spoke bluntly: "Today we reveal the truth behind the underground steroid market: dangerous drugs cooked up all too often in filthy conditions with no regard to safety, giving Americans who purchase them the ultimate raw deal."

CHAPTER SEVEN
TURNING A
BLIND EYE

German Olympic hurdler Anne-Kathrin Elbe had no idea she had been doping. Her coach, Thomas Springstein, had given PEDs to the runners he trained without explaining what the substances were. A teenager at the time she worked with Springstein, Elbe didn't learn the truth until years later, when Springstein faced prosecution for his actions in 2006. "He said that they were vitamins," said Elbe, still stunned a year after her former coach's trial.

Athletes don't always have a say in whether or not they use PEDs. Many place their trust in authority figures who pressure them to take unfamiliar substances, often without revealing the true nature of those substances. Coaches, team managers and owners, sports leagues, and even national and international federations can be driving forces in doping culture. By permitting, concealing, and in some cases actively promoting the use of banned substances among their athletes, these individuals and organizations bear a large share of the responsibility for doping in their sports.

"LIKE CANDY AT HALLOWEEN"

While some coaches assist athletes who want to dope, others provide banned substances to athletes without the athletes' knowledge, full understanding, or consent. In May 2014, retired US football players accused their former coaches and managers of doing just that. Former stars Richard Dent and Jim McMahon filed a class action suit against the NFL, charging that players received addictive painkilling drugs without proper prescriptions. The suit, which was eventually signed by twelve hundred retired players, also

German hurdler Anne-Kathrin Elbe, shown here at the 2006 Olympic Games, unknowingly ingested PEDs that her coach told her were vitamins.

claimed that dosages were too high, that drugs were "stacked" in unsafe combinations, that players' health was not monitored, and that no one told the players about the substances' serious side effects. Former players blame their excessive use of painkillers for a wide variety of health problems, including severe muscle pain, bone disease, impairment of nerves and vital organs, and addiction.

McMahon estimated that NFL doctors gave him "hundreds, if not thousands" of shots and pills. According to one player's lawyers, pills circulated freely in hotels and locker rooms "like candy at Halloween." The lawsuit further contended that team doctors wrote prescriptions in players' names without the players' knowledge. No one seemed worried about possible adverse reactions. On plane rides after games, trainers gave players medication even while they were consuming alcohol—an unsafe practice—with no objections from team doctors who were present.

In April 2014, a month after the suit was filed, a federal judge dismissed the lawsuit against the NFL—although the decision had nothing to do with the actual merits of the case, which were never debated. Judge William Alsup decided that the courts were not the proper place to sort through the players' grievances. He thought the issue should be resolved through collective bargaining, or direct negotiations between the players' representatives and NFL officials. Alsup also noted that the NFL requires teams and their owners to abide by health and safety measures. "This is not a situation in which the NFL has stood by and done nothing," he said. Rather, he indicated, the league's individual teams had independently hired doctors who allowed misconduct to take place. In other words, the actions described by Dent and McMahon were isolated incidents rather than part of an NFL-wide doping conspiracy.

Elsewhere in the sports world, however, doping cover-ups do involve the heads of athletic federations—and even officials working for anti-doping organizations. Working at the highest levels of their sport and in the heart of the anti-doping movement, top-ranking individuals can preside over a culture of doping that is rarely exposed to public view.

"TOP-SECRET DOPING"

Vitaly Stepanov found his ideal job as a doping control officer with the Russian Anti-Doping Agency (RUSADA). When he started working for RUSADA in 2007, Stepanov "wanted to make sports cleaner, more honest, better." Yuliya Rusanova, one of the world's top track-and-field athletes, met Stepanov in 2009—and what she confided shocked him. "During our first or second talk," he said, "she clearly told me that all athletes in Russia are doping."

Rusanova, who has since been banned from competition, went on record with her story in German journalist Hajo Seppelt's 2014 documentary, *Top-Secret Doping: How Russia Makes Its Winners.* Rusanova explained that the necessity for doping was taken for granted in high-level Russian athletics. "The coaches have it hammered into them and the coaches hammer it into the athletes," she told Seppelt. "Therefore, the athletes do not think when they are taking banned drugs that they are doing something illegal." Despite their divergent positions on doping, Stepanov and Rusanova fell in love and married. For a time, the anti-doping officer even helped his wife hide her use of performance enhancers. Eventually, however, they grew tired of lying and informed WADA of their situation. Speaking to Seppelt gave them a platform to take their message to the world.

The systematic doping depicted in Seppelt's documentary goes far beyond the couple's disclosures. One of the most dramatic revelations concerned Liliya Shobukhova, once considered "the best female marathon runner in the world," who admitted to paying the All-Russian Athletics Federation (ARAF) $550,000 to cover up her doping. The involvement of Valentin Balakhnichev, the president of ARAF, connected the scandal to an even larger anti-doping organization. At the time, Balakhnichev also served as the treasurer of the IAAF. Although he resigned both positions after being implicated in the Russian doping conspiracy, his actions cast suspicion on the IAAF as well as ARAF.

Years later, fresh evidence put the IAAF under even harsher scrutiny. In the summer of 2015, two scientists hired by German and British news agencies analyzed previously unpublished IAAF testing records and claimed that the IAAF had failed to investigate more than eight hundred suspicious blood samples between 2001 and 2012. Many of these samples came from Russian athletes. One scientist, Robin Parisotto, said, "Never have I seen such an alarmingly abnormal set of blood values. So many athletes appear to have doped with impunity, and . . . the IAAF appears to have idly sat by and let this happen." IAAF officials insisted that Parisotto and fellow scientist Michael Ashenden were misinterpreting sample data, calling their accusations "guesswork." Sebastian Coe, vice president of the IAAF, denied that the organization had handled its testing and follow-ups inappropriately. "There is nothing in our history of competence and integrity in drug testing that warrants this kind of attack," he said. Nevertheless, both the IAAF and WADA launched investigations into possible misconduct by IAAF employees.

CONFLICT OF INTEREST

All national and international athletic federations want to see their sport and their athletes thrive, but their position is complicated by their double role as enforcers of doping regulations and promoters of their sport. When an athlete tests positive for drugs, the organization governing the sport faces a conflict of interest. Officials sometimes fear that sanctioning the athlete will reflect poorly on the sport itself, causing the public to lose interest. For instance, throughout the late 1990s and early 2000s, UCI was aware of elite cyclists' use of performance enhancers but was willing to cover up anything that might harm their athletes' reputations or damage public confidence in the multimillion-dollar sport of cycling.

To protect the image of its athletes and its sport, UCI took extreme measures in 2005 when the French sports newspaper *L'Équipe* reported that Lance Armstrong had used EPO during the 1999 Tour de France. The evidence against Armstrong, which had been based on the retesting of an old sample alleged but not confirmed to be Armstrong's, could not be used to penalize him. The sample's results could, however, discredit his accomplishments and the sport in general. UCI immediately went on the defensive. Hoping to deflect WADA's investigation, UCI officials appointed a Dutch anti-doping expert, Emile Vrijman, to look into the matter. Instead of giving Vrijman free rein, however, UCI informed him that the "investigation must be clearly restricted." He could investigate how Armstrong's test results became public, but he could not comment on the results themselves. When Vrijman produced his report, UCI officials turned it over to Mark S. Levinstein, a well-known American sports lawyer who represented Armstrong. Levinstein's additions to the report included a good deal of material "highly critical" of WADA and the French anti-doping lab. The 2014 investigating commission concluded that UCI's "main goal was to ensure that the report reflected UCI's and Lance Armstrong's personal [rather than evidence-based] conclusions."

Professional cycling has changed in many ways since Armstrong and his doping teammates dominated the sport. UCI officials are eager to regain public confidence by acknowledging past mistakes and instituting reforms. In 2014 UCI appointed a three-member commission to investigate how well the union was handling its doping problem. The commissioners issued a harsh report, noting that they had interviewed athletes who admitted that PEDs were still part of cycling. Still, the commissioners concluded that "doping is either less prevalent today or that the nature of doping practices has changed such that the performance gains are smaller." In the current atmosphere, they believe "riders can now at least be competitive when riding clean."

"THE IDEAL SOLUTION"

While organizations such as Major League Baseball and UCI have worked to stop cheating and restore their images, some observers continue to question the wisdom of asking a sports federation to both promote its game and also police anti-doping policies. Is the tension between these priorities too much for officials to handle? British anti-doping official Michele Verroken thinks so. She supports criminalizing doping, which would give law enforcement and government agencies the power to prosecute dopers. "If we use criminal criteria we would create higher standards [for holding dopers accountable]," she contended in 2015. The issue is not a new one. In 2012 an interviewer asked former WADA president Dick Pound if he thought the responsibility for enforcing WADA regulations should be taken away from governing bodies such as federations and given to outside authorities. "I actually think the ideal solution is a [sports] governing body that is more interested in the purity and the integrity of its sport than . . . money," he maintained. Sports officials, he argued, are in the best position to know who is doping and how to catch them. The involvement of an outside agency would allow governing bodies to simply ignore doping since it would no longer be their concern. "In terms of dealing with the problem and managing it," he explained, "there ought to be nobody better than the sport itself."

Many athletes agree that real solutions to doping must come

Fans converge around Lance Armstrong after his unprecedented sixth Tour de France victory in 2004. Armstrong's star power brought cycling to international prominence and made cycling officials reluctant to pursue allegations of Armstrong's doping.

from within the athletic community. "I think there's got to be a real cast-iron will" to hold anti-doping officials accountable as well as athletes, said British track-and-field Olympic medalist Kriss Akabusi in 2015. "Let's go and chase the guys at the top, the big fish at the top, the guys that are making money out of it."

CHAPTER EIGHT
DOPING IN HIGH SCHOOLS

James Acton wanted to join his school's football team when he was a seventh grader in 1991. First, though, he had to have his parents sign a permission slip allowing his school to randomly test him for drugs. At the time, school officials in his hometown of Vernonia, Oregon, were aware of increased drug use among the student body and suspected athletes were among the major users. The drug-testing policy aimed to address the drug use problem in general and the higher risk of sports injuries among doping students in particular.

James and his parents, Wayne and Judy, believed the policy was unfair. A good student, James had never given anyone reason to suspect that he took drugs. His parents questioned why he should be subject to random testing. They claimed the policy violated his Fourth Amendment rights, which protect US citizens from "unreasonable searches and seizures." Not only did Wayne and Judy refuse to sign the permission form, they filed a lawsuit against the school district that went all the way to the Supreme Court. "Making kids take a drug test without any proof that they are taking drugs is just like searching a house without a warrant or proof of something wrong," James wrote in a press release weeks before the court decision in 1995.

A sharply divided Supreme Court ruled against the Actons, however. Presenting the majority opinion, Justice Antonin Scalia declared that the safety and well-being of students overrode the privacy issue. Some Americans hailed the ruling as a victory in the fight against drugs, while others condemned it as a blow to student privacy rights. President Bill Clinton applauded the decision as "send[ing] exactly the right message to parents and students: Drug use will not be tolerated in our schools."

GROWING PROBLEM

Instead of declining, however, the use of PEDs among US teenagers has continued to rise. According to a national survey released in 2014, 11 percent of students in ninth through twelfth grades admitted to having used synthetic HGH without a prescription. This represents a significant increase over figures for 2012, when only 5 percent said they had used the hormone. Steroid usage is also on the rise. According to a 2012 study, one in twenty teens has used steroids to develop muscle mass.

The reasons are varied. "There's the pressure to make the high school team," explained Annie Skinner of the USADA in 2014. "There's the pressure to do the best you can in high school to get that college scholarship, so the pressures on young athletes are very intense." In addition to sports performance, some teenagers look to drugs to improve their appearance. Often called "mirror athletes," these teens may not play a sport, but they want to see a strong, athletic figure when they look in the mirror.

The problem is compounded by a lack of regulation in both the manufacture and the sale of PEDs. "It's what you get when you combine aggressive promotion from for-profit [drug] companies with a vulnerable target—kids who want a quick fix and don't care about health risk," noted USADA president Travis Tygart in

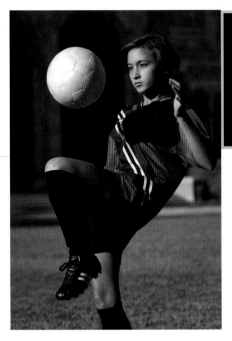

A growing number of teens in the United States admit to using steroids and human growth hormone without prescriptions, often in an effort to boost athletic performance.

2014. "It's a very easy sell, unfortunately." While legitimate drug companies promote their products as reliable performance boosters, underground providers are even more likely to draw in teenage customers. Because genuine HGH is expensive, black market sellers may offer cheaper, fake versions of the hormone. Whether young athletes purchase online, in a store, or from someone at school, they may not be getting what they think they are. The underground purchase exposes buyers to a range of risks due to impurities in the drug that may include toxic substances. Even authentic HGH can lead to stunted growth, acne, diabetes, liver problems, and other serious consequences when not used for a legitimate medical need.

A FAMILY'S GRIEF

No one is more aware of the dangers of doping than Don and Gwen Hooton. Their son Taylor was a bright, popular student athlete who pitched for his school's baseball team. In late 2002, he mentioned to a friend that he was considering taking steroids. When the friend wanted to know why, Taylor replied, "I'm not doing it for baseball. I'm

When the Biogenesis scandal emerged in 2013, the Florida community was shocked to learn that clinic owner Anthony Bosch had provided PEDs to teenagers as well as to elite athletes. The day after Bosch admitted his role in selling performance enhancers to high school students, the Miami-Dade school board announced the creation of a pilot program to test student athletes for steroids. Although limited funding will restrict the number of tests performed, school officials hope the program will discourage anyone thinking about doping. Also acknowledging the extent of the doping problem, the Florida High School Association passed new regulations. As of July 1, 2014, any student caught using HGH will be suspended from games. The same is true for any coach or school representative proven to have helped a student dope. "There's always an adult culprit behind these issues," said school superintendent Alberto Carvalho.

doing it for myself." Not long afterward, in 2003, Taylor's parents began to notice changes in their formerly genial son. He became easily annoyed and hostile. Angry outbursts were followed by tears and apologies. Sometimes Taylor pounded the floor in rage. On one occasion, he hit a wall so hard he injured his pitching hand. In incidents that were totally out of character, he stole money from his parents' bank account, as well as a camera and a laptop during a family vacation. On July 15, 2003, seventeen-year-old Taylor Hooton committed suicide. His father and the police found needles, syringes, and vials of steroids in his room. His parents and doctors believe that depression, brought on by withdrawal from steroids without medical supervision, caused his death.

Determined to honor their son and to raise public awareness of steroid abuse among teens, Don and Gwen Hooton established the Taylor Hooton Foundation in 2004. Since then Don Hooton has spoken with hundreds of thousands of teenagers, parents, coaches, medical professionals, and elite athletes. He has appeared on national and international television programs and shared his message of doping's dangers with newspapers and magazines.

When the US Congress investigated steroid use in Major League Baseball in 2005, Hooton went to Washington, DC, to testify before the House Committee on Government Reform. To Hooton's disappointment, however, the investigation did not result in any new programs to fight doping in high schools. Years later, in 2013, shortly before the tenth anniversary of his son's death, Hooton sent letters to every US senator and congressperson. "After all the

BETRAYAL

When MLB player Alex Rodriguez was implicated for using steroids in 2013, Don Hooton was shocked and saddened. Rodriguez had worked with the Taylor Hooton Foundation since 2009, speaking to groups of students on the dangers of performance enhancers. Hooton officially ended Rodriguez's connection to the foundation and refused the disgraced player's financial contributions. "To call it a betrayal is an understatement," said Hooton. "And you know what makes it such a shame? Alex did a wonderful job working for us. The kids loved him." Rodriguez has since called Hooton to apologize for the hurt he caused. The two men have agreed to shake hands if they meet again.

grandstanding before the TV cameras . . . our federal government has not instituted any form of education program for our children," he said. "It hasn't invested any time or effort in raising awareness about the scope of the problem. As a result, the steroid usage problem by our children has not gotten any better."

HIGH SCHOOL TESTING

In 2005, due in part to Hooton's tireless campaigning, New Jersey became the first state to create a statewide program to test high school athletes for steroids. Texas and Illinois followed suit within a few years. Although the legality of testing student athletes for drug use has been established, the effectiveness of such programs remains up for debate. Out of one thousand teenage athletes tested between 2006 and 2008 in New Jersey, only two tested positive for drugs. However, that figure almost certainly does not represent the actual number of students who are doping. School districts typically announce a schedule for drug testing, so student athletes know when they are most likely to be tested. Those who are doping can then figure out when to stop taking steroids or how to mask their use to produce negative test results. In particular, they can use the summer, rather than the school year, to bulk up since no tests are performed during the off-season. At a cost of $100,000 per year, New Jersey's program has faced questions about its usefulness. A single test can cost up to $300, a price that limits the number of athletes a school district can afford to test.

In fact, student testing programs are beset with so many problems and loopholes that the Texas legislature voted to end its program in the summer of 2015. The state had spent $10 million to test sixty-three thousand students over a six-year period. Despite the size of the program, very few individuals were caught doping—a result many blamed on loopholes in the testing. "While I am disappointed to see the testing program disappear, its demise was inevitable," said Don Hooton, who had originally advocated vigorously for the program. "The chances of this program catching one of our Texas high schoolers using steroids was somewhere between slim and none." Earlier that year, he had noted that he believed the program had done more harm than good. "Coaches, schools, and politicians have used the abysmal number of positive tests to prove there's no steroid problem. What did we do here? We just lulled the public to sleep."

Others have professed great confidence in high school testing programs despite the small number of positive tests. "We are trying to look out for the health and safety of our student-athletes," said Steven Timko, executive director of the New Jersey State Interscholastic Athletic Association. "I think we're trying to send the right message." Kurt Gibson, associate executive director of the Illinois High School Association, concurs. "[Testing is] another tool in the student's toolbox to say no to these substances," he explained. "Our program serves more as a deterrent rather than being designed to punish students."

EDUCATIONAL EFFORTS

If drug testing isn't the solution to teenage steroid use, what is? In 2008 anti-doping researcher Don Catlin suggested the use of biological passports, but this would require a great deal of time, expense, and medical involvement. Medical professionals would have to create a database to track students' test results over months and years. Most high school districts would find it difficult to assemble such resources, and parents and students might view the practice as an unwarranted invasion of privacy.

Many anti-doping advocates point to education as the most effective way to stem the rising use of PEDs among teens. Two particularly well-regarded programs are Athletes Training and Learning to Avoid Steroids (ATLAS) and Athletes Targeting Healthy

Exercise and Nutrition Alternatives (ATHENA). Created by Dr. Diane Elliot of Oregon Health and Sciences University in Portland, ATLAS works with young male athletes while ATHENA focuses on young women. Both programs incorporate role-playing and educational games to teach students how to attain their sports goals through nutrition and training. "They told us a ton of dangers that we did not even realize could be bad for our bodies," reported Amber Lease, a high school junior who participated in the program in 2015. Joey Lancaster, a senior from the same school, likewise noted that she "learned a lot about countless drugs. . . . It keeps me wanting to be safe and to have everything [be] natural."

Current and former professional athletes have also joined the effort to reach out to high school students about the dangers of doping. Cyclist Tyler Hamilton, who was once part of Lance Armstrong's cycling team, acknowledges that he had a lifelong ambition to win a gold medal. But when his dream came true in 2004, he was racked with guilt, knowing he had relied on PEDs to win. "It didn't feel anything like it was supposed to," Hamilton recalled. The cyclist was eventually forced to return the gold medal to the IOC after he admitted to using performance enhancers. "It felt better to give it back than it did to actually win it," he says. After his 2008 retirement from cycling, Hamilton began giving talks on behalf of the Partnership for Drug-Free Kids, traveling around the world to deliver his anti-doping message. "There's so much pressure on winning—it's tough for these kids to stay true to themselves," he said in 2014. "I can't change every kid's mind, but if I can do my part and other people do their part, we can beat this monster."

EPILOGUE
THE UNTOLD STORY

When Katherine Hamilton started college in 1979 at the University of California at Berkeley, she had all the makings of an athletic star. A heptathlete—one who competes in seven different running, jumping, and throwing events—she was the first woman to receive a four-year athletic scholarship in the school's track-and-field program. However, she soon found that many of her teammates were doping. Although Hamilton knew she would never dope, she also felt that with so many others taking steroids, she had no shot at being a top competitor. Rather than face what she considered a rigged system, she decided to give up sports altogether. Forfeiting her scholarship, she left school. Almost twenty-eight years later, in 2007, Hamilton was listening to a program about doping in sports on a National Public Radio talk show and called in to join the discussion. "There is an untold story," she told the listeners, "about all the thousands . . . [of] really great athletes doing the right thing, working really hard—and they just drop out because they're just not willing to do the things to your body [that dopers do] and go down that road."

Hamilton's experience reflects the prevalence of a doping culture that remains strong in many sports. British track-and-field champion Kriss Akabusi faced a similar culture but chose a different path. "When I was a young man, [in about] 1985 . . . someone suggested to me that if I really wanted to get better, then I'd have to consider alternative means. . . . I was able to have an informed decision and decide that wasn't the route for me." Akabusi went on to become a three-time Olympic medalist. Yet he acknowledges that the doping culture can frustrate many hardworking clean athletes, especially if

> **THOUSANDS . . . [OF] REALLY GREAT ATHLETES . . . [AREN'T] WILLING TO . . . GO DOWN THAT ROAD [OF DOPING].**
>
> KATHERINE HAMILTON

they learn that dopers have outperformed them. "It must be galling to turn around—ten, fifteen years later—and recognize that you should've had your day in the sun."

With athletes, doctors, trainers, coaches, drug providers, and even some anti-doping agents conspiring to protect the use of PEDs, and with some sports governing organizations failing to provide proper oversight, the use of banned substances may seem inevitable. Still, athletes and sports officials committed to clean competition refuse to give up. Olympic race walker Brendan Boyce of Ireland says he doesn't take drugs and doesn't dwell on the athletes who do. "I don't spend too much time thinking about [doping] because that produces a negative mind-set and you can't go out there thinking everyone's on drugs." Ranked ninth in the world in his sport as of 2015, Boyce believes he has a good chance at an Olympic or world championship medal while competing clean.

US Olympic track-and-field champion DeeDee Trotter takes

DeeDee Trotter (*left*) of the United States and Anastasiya Kapachinskaya (*right*) of Russia compete during the Women's 4 x 400-meter Relay Round 1 heats on Day 14 of the London 2012 Olympic Games at Olympic Stadium on August 10, 2012, in London, England.

a more active stance against doping. In 2006 she heard a fellow passenger on an airplane talking about the BALCO doping scandal. "This guy was reading the newspaper and he said 'Oh, they're all on drugs," Trotter recounted in 2012. "It really upset me that it's perceived that way—that if [an athlete] runs fast, then she's on drugs." Trotter decided she wouldn't tolerate this assumption. "I turned around and said, 'Hey—excuse me, I'm sorry, but that's not true. I'm a professional athlete and an Olympic gold medalist, and I'm not on drugs.'" The following year, Trotter founded Test Me I'm Clean, a nonprofit organization that works to educate athletes and the public about the dangers of PEDs and to promote drug-free athletics. Trotter also participates in USADA's Athlete Ambassador program, sharing her anti-doping message with students around the country.

WADA's current president, Sir Craig Reedie, aims to encourage such cooperation between athletes and anti-doping authorities. His goal is "to get everybody . . . working together, rather than to be telling people, 'You must do this or we will penalize you,'" he explains. Reedie feels that this collaborative approach, coupled with improved tests, promising research, and WADA's new stricter code will lead to major progress in the fight against doping. Even so, the clash between athletes on PEDs and anti-doping agencies shows no signs of abating. Both dopers and those pledged to stop them are determined to prevail in what has become the most high-stakes competition in sports.

TIMELINE

1904   Marathon runner Fred Lorz wins a gold medal in the first known instance of doping in the modern Olympics.

1950s   Dr. John Ziegler gives Dianabol to weight lifters.

1960   Cyclist Knud Jensen dies at the Rome Olympics after ingesting PEDs.

1965   The International Olympic Committee (IOC) establishes a medical commission to combat the use of PEDs.

1968   For the first time, an organized system of drug testing is put into effect at the Winter Olympics in Grenoble, France.

1960s–1980s   An enforced state-sponsored doping program in East Germany affects the lives of numerous young athletes.

1975   The IOC adds steroids to the list of banned substances after a test is developed to detect them.

1981   The Court of Arbitration for Sport (CAS) is established.

1980s   The steroid era of baseball begins. Many professional US baseball players take PEDs.

1988   Runner Ben Johnson becomes the first Olympic gold medalist to be stripped of his title after testing positive for PEDs.

1995   The US Supreme Court rules that schools have the right to require drug tests of student athletes.

1999   The IOC establishes the World Anti-Doping Agency (WADA).

1999   Lance Armstrong wins the Tour de France for the first time.

2003   A federal investigation of the Bay Area Laboratory Co-Operative (BALCO) summons dozens of athletes, including Marion Jones, to testify.

2004   The Taylor Hooton Foundation is established to educate teenagers on the dangers of steroids.

2005   UNESCO adopts the International Convention against Doping in Sport.

2007   The Mitchell Report implicates dozens of Major League Baseball players in doping.

2012   A USADA investigation concludes that Lance Armstrong relied on doping throughout his career.

2013   The Biogenesis doping scandal implicates dozens of Major League Baseball players, including Alex Rodriguez.

2014   A German television documentary reveals widespread doping among Russian athletes.

2015   Journalists accuse the International Association of Athletics Federations of ignoring evidence of doping among hundreds of athletes.

SOURCE NOTES

5 "Lance Armstrong's Interview with Oprah Winfrey: The Transcript," *Telegraph* (London), January 18, 2013, http://www.telegraph.co.uk /sport/othersports/cycling/lancearmstrong/9810801/Lance-Armstrongs -interview-with-Oprah-Winfrey-the-transcript.html.

5 Warner Todd Huston, "Lance Armstrong Refuses to Accept Tour de France Taking Titles Away," *Brietbart*, June 3, 2015, http://www.breitbart.com /sports/2015/06/03/lance-armstrong-refuses-to-accept-tour-de-france -taking-titles-away.

7 "Russian Doping Claims: 99% of Athletes Guilty, German TV Alleges," *BBC*, December 4, 2014, http://www.bbc.com/sport/0/athletics/30324812.

8 Matt Slater, "Doping in Cycling: Why Are the Amateurs 'Emulating the Pros'?," *BBC*, May 9, 2015, http://www.bbc.co.uk/sport/0 /cycling/32662773.

8 Andy Bull, "When Doctors Are Being Tempted to Cheat, Who Will Guard the Guardians?," *Guardian* (Manchester), February 15, 2013, http://www .theguardian.com/sport/2013/feb/15/drug-cheat-dilemma.

9 "Steroids Loom Large over Programs," *ESPN*, December 20, 2012, http:// espn.go.com/college-football/story/_/id/8765531/steroids-loom-major -college-football-report-says.

9 Brittany Stahl, "Despite MLB Scandals, Steroids Rampant in College Baseball," *NYU Journalism*, March 26, 2009, http://www.journalism.nyu .edu/publishing/archives/pavement/in/despite-mlb-scandals-steroids -rampant-in-college-baseball/index.html.

10 "A-Rod Admits, Regrets Use of PEDS," *ESPN*, February 10, 2009, http:// sports.espn.go.com/mlb/news/story?id=3894847.

10 Jason Mazanov, "The Lance Bomb Has Blown, but Is Doping Really Cheating?," in *Doping and Drugs in Sport*, vol. 364, ed. Justin Healey (Thirroul, NSW, Australia: Spinney, 2013), 37.

11 Michael Cook, "Should Olympic Athletes be Allowed to Use Performance-Enhancing Drugs?" in *Doping and Drugs in Sport*, vol. 364, ed. Justin Healey (Thirroul, NSW, Australia: Spinney, 2013), 31.

12 "'Performance-Enhancing' Drugs Decrease Performance," University of Adelaide, May 4, 2015, http://www.adelaide.edu.au/news/news77762 .html.

12 Helen Thompson, "Performance Enhancement: Superhuman Athletes," *Nature*, July 18, 2012, http://www.nature.com/news/performance -enhancement-superhuman-athletes-1.11029.

13 "Playing Through: Former and Current International Athletes of USADA," U.S. Anti-Doping Agency, accessed August 21, 2015, http://www.usada.org /playing-former-current-international-athletes-usada-2.

13 John J. MacAloon, *This Great Symbol: Pierre de Coubertin and the Origins of the Modern Olympic Games* (London: Routledge, 2013), xxv.

14 Karen Abbott, "The 1904 Olympic Marathon May Have Been the Strangest Ever," Smithsonian.com, August 12, 2012, http://www.smithsonianmag.com/history/the-1904-olympic-marathon-may-have-been-the-strangest-ever-14910747.

15 Thomas Hunt, *Drug Games: The International Olympic Committee and the Politics of Doping, 1960–2008* (Austin: University of Texas Press, 2011), 11.

15 Ibid. 10.

16 Justin Peters, "The Man behind the Juice," *Slate*, February 18, 2005, http://www.slate.com/articles/sports/sports_nut/2005/02/the_man_behind_the_juice.html.

17 Greg Downey, "Roid Age: Steroids in Sport and the Paradox of Pharmacological Puritanism," *PLOS*, July 9, 2012, http://blogs.plos.org/neuroanthropology/2012/07/09/roid-age-steroids-in-sport-and-the-paradox-of-pharmacological-puritanism.

17 Matthew Schofield, "East Germany's Doping Legacy Lives on, 25 Years Later," *McClatchy DC*, February 13, 2015, http://www.mcclatchydc.com/2015/02/13/256612/east-germanys-doping-legacy-lives.html.

18 Hunt, *Drug Games*, 7.

18 Ibid. 22.

19 David E. Newton, *Steroids and Doping in Sports: A Reference Handbook* (Santa Barbara, CA: ABC-CLIO, 2014), 73.

20 Hunt, *Drug Games*, 82.

21 Ibid. 83.

22 Jose Canseco, "Using Steroids in Baseball Is Beneficial to the Game," *Juiced: Wild Times, Rampant 'Roids, Smash Hits, and How Baseball Got Big*, in *Performance-Enhancing Drugs*, ed. Tamara L. Roleff (Detroit: Greenhaven, 2010), 67.

22 Ibid. 74.

23 "Mitchell Report: Baseball Slow to React to Players' Steroid Use," *ESPN*, December 14, 2007, http://sports.espn.go.com/mlb/news/story?id=3153509.

25 Hunt, *Drug Games*, 106.

26 John Christie, "Becky Scott Joins Top Level of WADA," *Globe and Mail* (London), September 17, 2012, http://www.theglobeandmail.com/sports/more-sports/becky-scott-joins-top-level-of-wada/article4550408.

30 Jesse Holland, "Floyd Mayweather Suggests Manny Pacquiao Is 'Slowly Changing' for Future 'Money' Fight," *SB Nation*, November 14, 2011, http://www.mmamania.com/2011/11/14/2561681/floyd-mayweather-suggests-manny-pacquiao-is-slowly-changing-for.

30 Ben Thompson, "Floyd Mayweather: 'Marquez Is Never Going to Get the Benefit of the Doubt," *Fight Hype*, November 14, 2011, http://www.fighthype.com/pages/content11193.html.

30 Greg Bishop, "Mayweather-Pacquiao Drug Testing Program Sets Precedent for Boxing," *Sports Illustrated*, last modified April, 22. 2015, http://www.si.com/boxing/2015/04/21/mayweather-pacquiao-drug-testing-us-anti-doping-agency-travis-tygart.

31 Ibid.

32 "Steroids Loom Large over Programs," *ESPN*, December 20, 2012, http://espn.go.com/college-football/story/_/id/8765531/steroids-loom-major-college-football-report-says.

34 Chris Cooper, *Run, Swim, Throw, Cheat: The Science behind Drugs in Sport*, (Oxford: Oxford University Press, 2012), 180.

39 "China Leads Government to Match IOC Anti-Doping Research Fund," World Anti-Doping Agency, September 4, 2014, https://www.wada-ama.org/en/media/news/2014-09/china-leads-government-commitment-to-match-ioc-anti-doping-research-fund.

41 Dick Pound, *Inside Dope: How Drugs Are the Biggest Threat to Sports, Why You Should Care, and What Can Be Done about Them* (Mississauga, ONT: John Willey & Sons, 2006), 40.

42 David A. Barron, David M. Martin, and Samir Abol Magd, "Doping in Sports and Its Spread to At-Risk Populations: An International Review," *World Psychiatry*, June 2007, http://www.ncbi.nlm.nih.gov/pmc/articles/PMC2219897.

46 Tim Franks, "Gene Doping: Sport's Biggest Battle?," *BBC News*, January 12, 2014, http://www.bbc.com/news/magazine-25687002.

46 Pound, *Inside Dope*. 44.

47 Gretchen Reynolds, "Outlaw DNA," *New York Times Magazine*, June 3, 2007, http://www.nytimes.com/2007/06/03/sports/playmagazine/0603play-hot.html?pagewanted=all&_r=0.

48 Sid Dorfman, "Lyle Alzado Remains the Reminder That Steroid Users Cheating Selves," *Newark (NJ) Star-Ledger*, August 13, 2013, http://www.nj.com/sports/ledger/dorfman/index.ssf/2013/08/lyle_alzado_a_reminder_that_st.html.

50 Ann Shipley, "Marion Jones Admits to Steroid Use," *Washington Post*, October 5, 2007, http://www.washingtonpost.com/wp-dyn/content/article/2007/10/04/AR2007100401666.html.

50 Duff Wilson, "After Five Years of Silence, Graham Says He Is Innocent of Doping," *New York Times*, October 24, 2009, http://www.nytimes.com/2009/10/25/sports/25graham.html.

52 Shipley, "Marion Jones Admits to Steroid Use."

52 Ibid.

53 M. Nicole Nazzaro, "Out of Track's Doping Scandal, Redemption and Progress," *New York Times*, August 17, 2013, http://www.nytimes.com/2013/08/18/sports/olympics/out-of-a-doping-scandal-redemption-for-Kelli-White-and-progress-for-track.html.

54 Christie Aschwanden, "The Top Athletes Looking for an Edge and the Scientists Trying to Stop Them," *Smithsonian Magazine*, July 2012, http://www.smithsonianmag.com/science-nature/the-top-athletes-looking-for-an-edge-and-the-scientists-trying-to-stop-them-138647491.

54 Pound, *Inside Dope*, 67.

56 Matt Slater, "Has the Biological Passport Delivered Clean or Confused Sport?," *BBC Sport*, November 12, 2014, http://www.bbc.com/sport/0/cycling/29959937.

57 Aschwanden, "The Top Athletes Looking for an Edge."

58 Slater, "Has the Biological Passport Delivered Clean or Confused Sport?"

59 Ibid.

62 Steve Eder, "Alex Rodriguez Told Federal Agents of Doping in Bosch Case, Report Says," *New York Times*, November 5, 2014, http://www.nytimes.com/2014/11/06/sports/baseball/alex-rodriguez-admits-to-doping-in-bosch-case.html?_r=0.

65 Sam Eifling, "Walk It Off, Champ," *Slate*, January 30, 2013, http://www.slate.com/articles/sports/sports_nut/2013/01/nfl_team_doctors_the_problem_with_pro_football_s_medical_sponsorship_deals.html.

66 Bull, "When Doctors Are Being Tempted to Cheat."

66 Ibid.

68 "Operation Juice Box: Fed Says Shelton Man Part of Steroids Dealing Network," *Shelton (CT) Herald*, May 5, 2015, http://www.sheltonherald.com/67891/feds-shelton-resident-was-part-of-illegal-steroids-dealing-network.

68 "32 Arrested and 2,000 Plants Seized in Marijuana Raid," United States Drug Enforcement Administration, December 8, 2005, http://www.dea.gov/pubs/states/newsrel/sanfran120805a.html.

69 Michael Schmidt, "U.S. Arrests 124 in Raids Global Steroid Ring," *New York Times*, September 24, 2007, http://www.nytimes.com/2007/09/24/sports/24cnd-steroid.html.

70 Reynolds, "Outlaw DNA."

72 "DEA Agents Surprise at Least 3 NFL Teams' Medical Staffs," *NPR*, November 17, 2014, http://www.npr.org/2014/11/17/364617212/dea -agents-surprise-at-least-3-nfl-teams-medical-staffs.

72 Rick Maese, "Federal Judge Dismisses NFL Painkiller Case," *Washington Post*, December 17, 2014, http://www.washingtonpost .com/sports/redskins/federal-judge-dismisses-nfl-painkiller -case/2014/12/17/3af89414-8630-11e4-abcf-5a3d7b3b20b8_story.html.

73 Hajo Seppelt, "English Script of the ARD-Documentary *Top-Secret Doping: How Russia Makes Its Winners*," December 2014, https://presse .wdr.de/plounge/tv/das_erste/2014/12/_pdf/English-Skript.pdf.

73 Ibid.

73 Ibid.

73 "Report: Russian Marathoner Shobukhova Paid to Avoid Doping Suspension," *Competitor.com*, December 3, 2014, http://running .competitor.com/2014/12/news/report-russian-marathoner-paid-avoid -doping-suspension_119094.

74 Dan Roan, "Leaked IAAF Doping Files: Wada 'Very Alarmed by Allegations," *BBC*, August 2, 2015, http://www.bbc.com/sport/0 /athletics/33749208.

74 "Doping Allegations a 'Declaration of War' on Athletics—Lord Coe," *BBC*, August 5, 2015, http://www.bbc.com/sport/0/athletics/33784236.

75 Ian Austen, "Report Says Doping Was Ignored to Shield Armstrong," *New York Times*, March 8, 2015, http://www.nytimes.com/2015/03/09/sports /cycling/cycling-union-ignored-doping-and-protected-lance-armstrong -commission-finds.html?_r=0.

75 Ibid.

76 Ibid.

76 Craig Lord, "Time to Take Doping into the Realms of Criminality of Fight to Be Won—Verroken," *SwimVortex.com*, March 24, 2015, http://www .swimvortex.com/time-to-take-doping-into-the-realms-of-criminality-if -fight-to-be-won-says-verroken.

76 "Richard Pound Interview," interviewed by Shane Stokes, *Velonation*, October 5, 2012, http://www.velonation.com/News/ID/12997/Richard -Pound-Interview-The-Kimmage-case-Armstrong-the-governance-of -cycling-and-more.aspx.

77 "Kriss Akabusi: Someone Suggested I Consider Doping," *BBC*, August 3, 2014, http://www.bbc.co.uk/programmes/p02yq1jz.

78 "Bill of Rights," *The Charters of Freedom*, accessed August 17, 2015, http://www.archives.gov/exhibits/charters/bill_of_rights_transcript.html.

78 Lyle Denniston, "Supreme Court to Rule on Drug Testing," *Baltimore Sun*, March 27, 1995, http://articles.baltimoresun.com/1995-03-27 /news/1995086032_1_drug-testing-random-drug-taking-drugs.

79 "School Drug Tests: Right or Wrong? Many Schools Could Begin Drug Tests on Athletes after Supreme Court Ruling," *Current Events* 95, no. 2, September 11, 1995, available online at http://www.loyno.edu/~wagues /article7.html.

79 Alexandra Pannoni, "Doping Rises among High Schoolers, but Few Districts Test," *U.S. News and World Report*, August 11, 2014, http://www .usnews.com/education/blogs/high-school-notes/2014/08/11/testing-high -school-athletes-for-doping-uncommon.

80 "Growth Hormone Use Exploding among High School Teens," *New York Post*, July 23, 2014, http://nypost.com/2014/07/23/growth-hormone-use -exploding-among-high-school-teens.

81 "Miami-Dade Schools Plan Steroid Testing Program," Taylor Hooton Foundation, August 7, 2014, http://taylorhooton.org/miami-dade-schools -plan-steroid-testing-program.

81 "Real Stories," *Taylor Hooton Foundation*, accessed February 20, 2015, http://taylorhooton.org/real-stories.

82 Wayne Coffey, "Taylor Hooton Foundation Refuses Check from Alex Rodriguez, Ready to Move on Without Him," *New York Daily News*, November 16, 2014, http://www.nydailynews.com/sports/baseball /yankees/coffey-hooton-fight-peds-a-rod-article-1.2013137.

83 Eden Stiffman, "10 Years after Son's Death, McKinney Father Still Fighting Youth Steroid Use," *Dallas Morning News*, August 16, 2013, http://www.dallasnews.com/news/community-news/mckinney /headlines/20130816-ten-years-after-sons-death-father-still-fighting -youth-steroid-use.ece.

84 Jim Vertuno, "Texas Votes to End High School Steroid Testing," *Huffington Post*, June 1, 2015, http://www.huffingtonpost.com/2015/06/01/texas -high-school-steroid-testing_n_7485704.html.

84 "Texas Ready to Dump High School Steroids Testing Program," *New York Times*, March 20, 2015, http://www.nytimes.com/aponline/2015/03/20 /us/ap-us-texas-high-school-steroids.html.

84 Mary Pilon, "Differing Views on Value of High School Tests," *New York Times*, January 5, 2013, http://www.nytimes.com/2013/01/06/sports /drug-tests-for-high-school-athletes-fuel-debate.html?_r=0.

85 Joaquin Aguilar, "Student Athletes Learn Dangers of Performance-Enhancing Drugs," *Klamath Falls (OR) Herald and News*, March 27, 2015, http://www.heraldandnews.com/news/local_news/student-athletes-learn -dangers-of-performance-enhancing-drugs/article_0e1bb6f8-d449-11e4 -81c6-2f55fe72d2aa.html.

85 Christian Red, "Disgraced Cyclist Tyler Hamilton Talks with Daily News about How He Brings Anti-Drug Message to Kids," *New York Daily News*, August 9, 2014, http://www.nydailynews.com/sports/more -sports/disgraced-cyclist-tyler-hamilton-brings-anti-drug-message-kids -article-1.1897986.

85 "Growth Hormone Use Exploding among High School Teens," *New York Post*.

86 Tom Goldman, "Athlete's 'Nope to Dope' Became 'No to Sports,'" *NPR*, August 30, 2010, http://www.npr.org/templates/story/story .php?storyId=129533093.

87 "Kriss Akabusi," *BBC*.

88 "You Can't Go Out There Thinking Everyone's on Drugs," *The42.ie*, March 28, 2015, http://www.the42.ie/brendan-boyce-race-walker-2011968 -Mar2015.

89 Aschwanden, "The Top Athletes Looking for an Edge."

89 Ben Rumsby, "New Wada President Sir Craid Reedie Reveals How He Will Tackle the Growing Problem of Drug Cheats," *Telegraph* (London), November 16, 2013, http://www.telegraph.co.uk/sport/othersports /drugsinsport/10453984/New-Wada-president-Sir-Craig-Reedie-reveals -how-he-will-tackle-the-growing-problem-of-drug-cheats.html.

GLOSSARY

anabolic steroids: hormones that promote muscle growth

arbitration: the settling of a dispute by an officially appointed, independent person or body

beta2-agonists: bronchodilator medications, used with asthma patients, that open air passages and increase the flow of oxygen

biological passport: a record of biological findings taken over a period of time and used to detect changes that may indicate doping

blood doping: manipulation of the blood to boost an athlete's number of oxygen-carrying red blood cells, often taking the form of a transfusion from a matched donor or from the athlete's own stored blood

deoxyribonucleic acid (DNA): a substance in a body's cells that carries genetic information

diuretic: medication that increases the production of urine and flushes other substances from the body

epitestosterone: a natural hormone that exists in balance with testosterone

erythropoietin (EPO): a hormone that increases the production of red blood cells

gene doping: an attempt to gain an athletic advantage through genetic manipulation, such as inserting a gene into the DNA

hormone: a naturally occurring substance in the body that doping athletes often ingest in synthetic form to increase endurance

human growth hormone (HGH): hormone used by athletes to increase muscle mass

masking agent: a substance used to mask or hide an athlete's use of performance-enhancing drugs

out-of-competition testing: unannounced tests for performance enhancers during training and off-season periods

performance-enhancing drug (PED): a natural or artificial substance ingested to boost strength and endurance or to increase muscle mass

plasma expander: a substance that increases the plasma, or liquid portion of the blood

reticulocyte: a newly produced red blood cell

stimulant: a substance that boosts energy and alertness

testosterone: a natural male hormone that boosts strength and muscle mass

tribunal: an institution with the authority to judge claims and disputes

SELECTED BIBLIOGRAPHY

"An Athlete's Dangerous Experiment." Taylor Hooton Foundation. Accessed March 31, 2015. http://taylorhooton.org/taylor-hooton.

Austen, Ian. "Report Says Doping Was Ignored to Shield Armstrong." *New York Times*, March 8, 2015. http://www.nytimes.com/2015/03/09/sports /cycling/cycling-union-ignored-doping-and-protected-lance-armstrong -commission-finds.html?_r=0.

Cooper, Chris. *Run, Swim, Throw, Cheat: The Science behind Drugs in Sport*. Oxford: Oxford University Press, 2012.

Eder, Steve. "Alex Rodriguez Told Federal Agents of Doping in Bosch Case, Report Says." *New York Times*, November 5, 2014. http://www.nytimes .com/2014/11/06/sports/baseball/alex-rodriguez-admits-to-doping-in -bosch-case.html?_r=0.

Elfrink, Tim, and Gus Garcia-Roberts. *Blood Sport: Alex Rodriguez, Biogenesis, and the Quest to End Baseball's Steroid Era*. New York: Dutton, 2014.

Healey, Justin, ed. *Doping in Sports*. Vol. 364. Thirroul, NSW, Australia: Spinney, 2013.

Hunt, Darren. "Keeping Performance Enhancing Drugs from High Schoolers." *ABC, Kvia.com*, August 6, 2014. http://www.kvia.com/news/keeping -performance-enhancing-drugs-from-high-schoolers/27333702.

Hunt, Thomas M. *Drug Games: The International Olympic Committee and the Politics of Doping, 1960–2008*. Austin: University of Texas Press, 2011.

Macur, Juliet. *Cycle of Lies: The Fall of Lance Armstrong*. New York: HarperCollins, 2014.

Pannoni, Alexandra. "Doping Rises among High Schoolers, but Few Districts Test." *U.S. News and World Report*, August 11, 2014. http://www.usnews .com/education/blogs/high-school-notes/2014/08/11/testing-high-school -athletes-for-doping-uncommon.

Pelley, Scott, corr. "The Case of Alex Rodriguez." *CBS News, 60 Minutes*. Aired on January 12, 2014. http://www.cbsnews.com/news/the-case-of-alex -rodriguez.

Pilon, Mary. "Differing Views on Value of High School Tests." *New York Times*, January 5, 2013. http://www.nytimes.com/2013/01/06/sports/drug-tests -for-high-school-athletes-fuel-debate.html.

Pound, Dick. *Inside Dope: How Drugs Are the Biggest Threat to Sports, Why You Should Care, and What Can Be Done about Them*. Mississauga, ONT: John Wiley and Sons, 2006.

————— *Inside the Olympics: A Behind-the-Scenes Look at the Politics, the Scandals, and the Glory of the Games*. Mississauga, ONT: John Wiley and Sons, 2004.

Quinn, T. J. "A Hopeless Battle Worth Fighting." *ESPN*, November 20, 2012. http://espn.go.com/espn/otl/story/_/id/8655313/wada-david-howman -discusses-state-doping-ped-policing-major-sports?src=mobile.

Reynolds, Gretchen. "Phys Ed: Will Olympic Athletes Dope If They Know It Might Kill Them?" *New York Times*, January 21, 2010. http://well.blogs .nytimes.com/2010/01/20/phys-ed-will-olympic-athletes-dope-if-they -know-it-might-kill-them.

Roleff, Tamara L., ed. *Performance-Enhancing Drugs*. Detroit: Greenhaven, 2010.

Seppelt, Hajo, narr. English script of the ARD-documentary *Top-Secret Doping: How Russia Makes Its Winners*. Broadcast in Germany, December 2014. https://presse.wdr.de/plounge/tv/das_erste/2014/12/_pdf/English-Skript .pdf.

Stiffman, Eden. "10 Years after Son's Death, McKinney Father Still Fighting Youth Steroid Use." *Dallas Morning News*, August 16, 2013. http://www .dallasnews.com/news/community-news/mckinney/headlines/20130816 -ten-years-after-sons-death-father-still-fighting-youth-steroid-use.ece.

Thompson, Helen. "Performance Enhancement: Superhuman Athletes." *Nature*, July 18, 2012. http://www.nature.com/news/performance -enhancement-superhuman-athletes-1.11029.

Ungerleider, Steven. *Faust's Gold: Inside the East German Doping Machine*. New York: Thomas Dunne Books, 2001.

Vigneron, Peter. "Why the Russian Runner Doping Scandal Matters." *Outside*, December 15, 2014. http://www.outsideonline.com/1928046/why -russian-runner-doping-scandal-matters.

Wick, Jeannette Y. "Performance-Enhancing Drugs: A New Reality in Sports?" *Pharmacy Times*, March 13, 2014. http://www.pharmacytimes.com /publications/issue/2014/March2014/Performance-Enhancing-Drugs-A -New-Reality-in-Sports.

Zaccagna, Remo. "Number of Cheaters Diminishing, Pound Says." *Halifax (NS) Chronicle Herald*, March 12, 2015. http://thechronicleherald.ca /sports/1274359-number-of-cheaters-diminishing-pound-says.

FURTHER INFORMATION

Books

Goldsmith, Connie. *Dietary Supplements: Harmless, Helpful, or Hurtful?* Minneapolis: Twenty-First Century Books, 2016. Learn more about the health risks posed by a range of substances, including sports supplements.

Hile, Lori. *Getting Ahead: Drugs, Technology, and the Competitive Advantage*. Portsmouth, NH: Heinemann, 2012. Read case studies that examine the choices and technologies driving athletes to dope.

Parks, Peggy J. *Drugs and Sports*. San Diego: Reference Point, 2010. Discover more about PED statistics, viewpoints, and testing policies for students and professional athletes.

Websites

Play True Generation
https://www.wada-ama.org/en/what-we-do/education-awareness/play-true-generation
This computer game, developed by WADA, covers the dangers of doping and the benefits of good nutrition and proper training.

Taylor Hooton Foundation
http://taylorhooton.org
The website presents news articles about APEDs and real-life stories about young athletes, including Taylor Hooton's tragedy.

United States Anti-Doping Agency
http://www.usada.org
Find more information on anti-doping testing, science and research, and education programs.

World Anti-Doping Agency
https://www.wada-ama.org
The website includes materials about banned substances, the testing process, and how WADA operates.

Youth Olympic Games
http://www.olympic.org/youth-olympic-games
Read stories and news about the Youth Olympic Games and some of its star athletes.

Film

Secrets of the Dead: Doping for Gold. DVD. Directed and produced by Alison Rooper. Narrated by Liv Schreiber. New York: PBS Home Video, 2008.

INDEX

PHOTO ACKNOWLEDGMENTS

The images in this book are used with the permission of: © iStockphoto .com/P_Wei, p. 6; © Jack Mitchell/Getty Images, p. 16; © Mike Powell/Getty Images, p. 20; © Rich Pilling/MLB Photos/Getty Images, p. 23; REUTERS/ Lyle Stafford/Newscom, p. 27; © Fabrice Coffrini/AFP/Getty Images, p. 28; © Joseph Agcaoili/AFP/Getty Images, p. 31; © Mark J. Terrill/AP/Corbis, p. 34; AP Photo/Rick Rycroft, p. 41; © Anne Cusack/Los Angeles Times/ Getty Images, p. 45; Se-Jin Lee and Alexandra C. McPherron/Department of Molecular Biology and Genetics/Johns Hopkins University School of Medicine, p. 47; © Matt Turner/Getty Images, p. 51; AP Photo/Paul Sakuma, p. 53; © Robert Lachman/Los Angeles Times/Getty Images, p. 63; © Lucas Oleniuk/ Toronto Star/Getty Images, p. 66; © Andy Lyon/Getty Images, p. 71; © AFP PHOTO/POOL/L'EQUIPE/Getty Images, p. 77; © iStockphoto.com/EHStock, p. 80; © Quinn Rooney/Getty Images, p. 89.

Front cover: © iStockphoto.com/vuk8691.
Back cover: © iStockphoto.com/Michael Krinke.

ABOUT THE AUTHOR

Stephanie Sammartino McPherson wrote her first children's story in college. She enjoyed the process so much that she's never stopped writing. A former teacher and freelance newspaper writer, she is the author of many books and numerous magazine stories. She especially enjoys writing about science and the human interest stories behind major discoveries. Her recent books include *Arctic Thaw: Climate Change and the Global Race for Energy Resources* and the award-winning *Iceberg, Right Ahead: The Tragedy of the Titanic*, an ALA Notable Children's Book. She and her husband, Richard, live in Virginia but also call California home.